Timeless Ripples

Timeless Ripples

The Kingdom of the Son of Man

WANG BIN YU

RESOURCE *Publications* · Eugene, Oregon

TIMELESS RIPPLES
The Kingdom of the Son of Man

Resource Publications
An Imprint of Wipf and Stock Publishers
199 W. 8th Ave., Suite 3
Eugene, OR 97401

www.wipfandstock.com

PAPERBACK ISBN: 978-1-5326-9977-1
HARDCOVER ISBN: 978-1-5326-9978-8
EBOOK ISBN: 978-1-5326-9979-5

Manufactured in the U.S.A.   04/18/19

To Binbin,
my heavenly Muse

Contents

Introduction

THIS STORY IS ABOUT the Son of Man, the most-human of humans. Wisdom tells us that it is disingenuous to try to be like someone else, but this does not apply to the Son of Man—for we are only ourselves when we become like him. This story is, therefore, also about us.

We become ourselves as we rub shoulders with others, when we become aware that helping them is inseparable from our own pilgrimages. As we find our way, we encounter countless others who are similarly finding their ways. The pilgrimage that we are on may thus be likened to two rocks tossed into a pond, the ripples of which intersect with each other.

Early believers referred to the Son of Man as the Rock. Because individuals typically love themselves more than anything else, they have been prone to cast away this Rock. As ugly as it may be, however, such casting has often produced beauty. This should not surprise us, though, for beauty is often made from ugliness—"the stone that the builders rejected has become the chief cornerstone."

What holds for individuals, is also true of entire nations. The Son of Man likened the kingdom of God to a small seed that grows into a massive tree. The growth of the seed is indiscernible because it takes place under the soil; but it grows into a massive tree, upon which the birds of the air perch. Like the seed, individuals and entire nations grow in the kingdom as they follow the teachings of the Son of Man.

This Son of Man (who was first referred to as the Seed of the Woman), similarly did not have an impressive beginning. While he germinated in lifeless soil, life has come out of his teachings and even his death. His lineage includes four disreputable women: Tamar seduced her father-in-law Judah, Rahab was a prostitute, Ruth enticed Obed on a threshing floor, and Bathsheba forcibly lay with King David. For those who have ears to hear, however, beauty has come through such lowliness—even through the *cry of a tiny babe*.[1]

---

1. Bruce Cockburn, "Cry of a Tiny Babe" (song)

Vignette 1

A Letter from Felix

DEAR WIFE:

Greetings. I have not written to you for many months. I have wanted to do so, but I have been kept busy.

As you know, years ago I was sent by Rome to keep the peace. My first post was in Bethlehem. Because of my competence, I was promoted. I am now in Jerusalem. (I previously told you about this possibility—the gods have been so good to us.)

Since coming to Jerusalem, I have learned much about the world and myself.

With regard to the world, many battles have been fought in this area. (I don't know why empires fought over this desolate land; it must have been for strategic purposes.) I am only here because it is the will of Rome. I dare say that most of my friends would say the same thing.

Judea is hard to control, mostly because of its ungrateful inhabitants. The peace of Rome has come to them—roads, aqueducts, ports, amphitheaters, and countless other things besides. But this has not satisfied the Jews, for above all else they have wanted us to respect their religion—and any sensible person would say we have done just that. We built them a temple for their god; but they did not like to see any Roman presence in the temple area—not even the Roman insignia. Ungrateful wretches! The temple only exists because of Roman generosity. (I myself think that building the temple was a mistake, for it has become the locus around which many sects squabble.)

What is more, many Jews have encouraged rebellion. Out of sheer lunacy, some have even contended that their god "anointed" them to fight against Rome. The most recent lunatic is a man from the north, whose name is Jesus. I must say, however, that he is wiser than others—others who have said that Rome must be overthrown militarily so that Judea might be governed by the "messiah." Jesus has been wiser, for he teaches that another kingdom exists, a kingdom that will succeed not through power but through weakness. I have no doubt that Jesus only says this because he wants what other twisted minds want; but unlike them, he is a realist, for he knows that his kingdom could never overpower the world.

My contention that the ultimate plan of Jesus is to overthrow Rome is partly based on his now famous teaching: "Give to Caesar what is Caesar's, and give to God what is God's." What Jesus fails to realize is that giving to Caesar is to give to God. The attempt of Jesus to build a kingdom of love that will overthrow Rome is nonsensical—for love ("peace" is the word that I use) comes only through Caesar. Caesar is Lord. Caesar is the King of kings. The man responsible for bringing Jesus into the world ought to have his throat slit!

I said above that I am learning both about the world and myself.

With regard to myself, I think that I now have a good idea of what people are really about. Because I am clever, I can see through their pretenses and displays.

I am also starting to learn more about what "peace" means. When I talk of the "peace of Rome," I no longer think in a strictly literal way (building roads, ports, aqueducts, and the like). The word "peace" presupposes the timeless universal Good—such that someone from the present may access the same reservoir that someone from the future accesses (be they poets, bards, historians, or playwrights). All that matters is growing in the universal Good; every other endeavor is meaningless. Thankfully, we are already instruments of Goodness, for anyone who seeks the Good worships Caesar.

(I recently had such thinking in mind when I mockingly asked two competing rabbis if either of them could recite the whole of their holy book while standing on one leg. Much to my surprise, one of them stood on one leg and said something like, "Love god with everything that you are, and love your neighbor as yourself; everything else in scripture is commentary." What I have said about the Good being timeless is akin to what this rabbi said about the central teaching of his holy book: all humanity has a general understanding of truth—but practicing such truth may be quite another matter.)

In any case, I don't have time to reflect on this matter sufficiently—especially so because I have to deal with lunatics.

Should the gods allow it, I will be home next summer.

Greet my friends and relatives. Greet our son Marcus. Encourage him to forgive me. How is our daughter Photis doing? I hope that she is managing well—even in spite of the pain that her limp brings.

Your faithful husband,

FELIX

Vignette 2

Mary the Virgin, and a Harlot

MARY THE MOTHER OF Jesus befriended a harlot. She did not judge this woman as others did, for she herself was pregnant without having been wed. Mary first met this woman as they were drawing water from a deep well—which was fed by the River Lethe.

The woman bluntly asked, "Will you marry Joseph because he knocked you up?" Mary sullenly replied: "Joseph is not the father, for we have not made love." The woman continued in her aggressive manner: "Then who is the father? Perhaps you have lain with many men and you don't know which one is the father." Mary insisted that she had not even been caressed by a man, much less had sex.

Thinking that Mary was now showing colors of self-righteousness, the woman indignantly queried: "Are you saying that *you are growing a child without the help of a man*?"[1] Mary was taken aback by the question, even as the woman mockingly declared, "*Hail Mary! Blessed is the fruit of your womb!*"[2]

Seeing that Mary did not retaliate, the woman calmed down a little.

"Come on, Mary, you know that you spread your legs for a man—whether willingly or unwillingly. Maybe the people are right: maybe a Roman soldier raped you, and now you are ashamed. The people are wrong in judging you—even as those hypocrites are wrong in judging me. You did not enjoy the experience. I understand. Men satisfied my need for money, but my desire for love has never been met."

The woman's rant then became confused and disjointed. While she was incensed at the seeming self-righteousness of Mary, she also, oddly enough, felt that Mary understood her. She was partially correct, for Mary was empathetic—even as she often asked herself, "who am I?"

"I don't know the names of most of the men that I have had sex with," the woman continued. "I of course know the name of my father, who forced me when I was too young to protest (he said that *he could do what he wanted with his possessions*).[3] I also know the names of several prominent men; but the encounters were all impersonal—such men only wanted to get off."

What the woman had said hurt Mary, but because she knew that the woman had interpreted Mary's circumstance through her own sordid tale, Mary forgave her. Mary was this way toward all who abused her—almost to the point of forgetting how she had been wronged.

Vignette 3

Melchior, the Magus

TOGETHER WITH OTHER MAGI, Melchior left his country to see the child who was slated to bring peace. Melchior said that he was on a spiritual quest. At one level, this proved to be true; but at the time Melchior was not being honest with himself, for he was using the trek to Bethlehem as a pretext to avoid his troubles. Melchior was thus no different than most other pilgrims—people who have the best of intentions in journeying towards the kingdom, but who are nevertheless beset by cloudy understandings of goodness.

At first, Melchior thought that things would become better as he neared Judea; but he found just the opposite to be true. The further he travelled, the darker things seemed to be, such that he wondered if he was travelling *to witness a sacred birth or his own death*.[4] (The pilgrimage of Melchior really did not begin with setting out, but with this wondering.) Things took on an abhorrent hue: the food was unpalatable, his servants were like savages, and even the camels seemed to stink more than they really did. Little things also irritated him—how bundles were tied, how fires were lit, and how his men seemed to have an insatiable thirst for wenches and wine. Augmenting his anger was the growing hatred that Melchior had of himself, for he saw the squalor of the world within himself: at every turn and at every village, it was like looking in a mirror. Melchior then prided himself in the fact that he alone knew that the same darkness that was within others was also in him—but this pride made his life yet more loathsome. Melchior wanted to die. ("Why," he would ask with the prophet, "did I ever leave my mother's womb only to see hardship?") Death did come to Melchior, but not in the way that he had wished—for while he wanted to die quickly and without undue suffering, death came to him as slowly as undulating sand dunes.

At the end of each day, Melchior liked to sit around the campfire and listen to stories. Melchior was particularly fond of listening to his cook, for the cook seamlessly wove tales together in such a way that one never knew where another person's story left off and where the cook's story began. Some of the others who sat around the campfire jadedly referred to the cook as a liar. While Melchior was aware of the cook's tendency to tell the stories of others as if they were his own, he nevertheless enjoyed the stories, which were always charged with imagination.

One story that the cook told concerned an island inhabited by women who made beautiful music. "On one of my voyages," the cook said, "the ship that I was aboard was nearing an island from which beautiful music emanated. I had heard that ships that approached this island did so to their own peril, for the music had a spell within it that drove sailors mad with lust—a lust that could not be satisfied but only fed by going closer to the island. Precisely what happened to the sailors is unknown, but they were never heard from again. Knowing this story saved me. Seeing that the captain and other sailors only mocked my warnings of the impending doom, I told them that they could have all my money if only they would tie my arms down in the raft and set me adrift. (I reasoned that binding my arms would keep me from rowing to the island and that I would have better chances in the open sea than if I succumbed to that lusty music.) Alas! My warnings vindicated themselves . . . " Not wanting to hear any more, the servant of another magi interrupted the cook and accused him of plagiarism: "You are a thief, for the story that you recounted was first penned by Homer about Ulysees. No doubt, you cleverly twisted the particulars of the story: where, for instance, Ulysees had himself tethered to the mast, you had yourself bound to a raft. All the same, it is the same story, yet you pretend that it is your own." The cook retorted by saying, "I know nothing about Omer or OOlysees. I swear by the shield of Hercules and all that is holy that the story is my own. I still have the scars from struggling with the ropes that bound me; and I still hear echoes of the seductive music. Perhaps OOlysees experienced the same thing that I experienced. Indeed, why do you find it odd that people might have similar stories?" Lest the exchange should become more heated, Melchior then stepped in. Melchior asked the cook how he managed to escape the ordeal. Only too glad to continue his tale, the cook said, "After I freed myself from my bonds, and with the stars as my guides, I rowed the boat to safety."

Melchior reflected on the heated exchange over the coming days and weeks. Like the ebbing and flowing of waves, his thoughts came and just as quickly left. It seemed to Melchior that he reflected well up until a rude interruption came his way—perhaps the cussing of servants, an annoying insect, or the stagger of his camel.

One of Melchior's first reflections concerned the honesty of the cook. While, Melchior thought to himself, "I do not appreciate untruth, I nevertheless think that more destructive to the soul than telling a lie is the thinking that one can recount a story without, at the same time, interpreting it. Every telling is a retelling replete with interpretation. Thinking otherwise is as mythical as the siren story, or even the story of the wise men who . . ." But just as Melchior was reflecting on this, he started to tip over in his saddle (the buckle of which had lost its strength). As he struggled to straighten up, a grain of sand then dared to land in his eye—as if the grain had a will of its own. Things and circumstances knew what they were doing, and Melchior felt right in hating them. Melchior then muttered to himself: *"Everything is against you. The weather is against you, the dirt is against you, and your servants are against you. They're all in league against you."*[5] After Melchior managed to sit aright once more and maintain his composure, he resumed his reflections. "While the cook," he thought, "needs to know that he tells the stories of others as if he himself was in them, I nevertheless applaud him for having an autobiographical view of life, for the stories of others are our stories, and we only know ourselves when we know others. (I abhor the thinking of those who accused the cook of plagiarism—the road to Hades is, indeed, often paved with such 'honesty') . . ." Just at that moment, the saddle of Melchior was completely undone. Losing all dignity and inner quietude, he fell to the sand together with some baggage—even as the camel snorted in disapproval. Melchior immediately felt the need to blame someone. In a fit of rage, he insulted the baggage handler—who was unable to defend himself because of a stuttering problem. Melchior was nevertheless demanding. "Why," he loudly barked (supposing that the stutterer was deaf), "did the saddle fall from the camel?" The servant *tried to speak but he could not say*: "I . . . I am . . . s . . . sor . . . sorry."[6] No, the saddle should not have fallen off the camel. Melchior was dead right, but dead all the same.

After the saddle was securely fastened with fresh throngs, Melchior mounted the camel and resumed the journey. *"Where was I?"* he asked himself; "*oh yes . . . this camel . . . that sand . . . this interpretation.*[7] I don't know exactly where I was or where I was going," he went on, "but I should now reflect on how I reflect on the interruptions. Interruptions are the very fabric of life. Removing them is akin to trying to take a single thread from the blanket under my saddle with the hope that doing so will not compromise the whole blanket. Everything is tied to everything else—the camel's eye cannot say to its stinky foot, 'I don't need you.' Given that everything is tied to everything else in a grand fabric, and given that the stories of others can become my story, it follows that I must choose what story I want to inhabit. Not choosing a story is, itself, to choose the story of nothingness. Like the cook, I am a sailor lost at sea, and like him, I am looking for a star." As Melchior continued his esoteric ruminations, the constant up and down movement of the camel caused him to feel the calling of nature—but, dignified man that he was (though less than completely forthright), he told his servants to find a campsite quickly.

When he at last had time to reflect more sufficiently on interruptions, Melchior found that it was not just circumstances that interrupted him, but even thought itself. Even positive thoughts distracted his attention away from his reflections. An old memory, for instance, came to him about how he had played with his daughter. After they had fun placing blocks on top of each other, the two of them started to put the blocks back into a pail. The little girl, who was a toddler at the time, did not understand that she needed to drop the blocks directly over the pail if they were to fall into it. Melchior laughed nervously as he recalled that she became angry at the blocks because they would not do what she wanted them to do. Another memory then came to him. He remembered how frantic his daughter became when she saw her mother preparing to feed her, and then how peaceful she became when her tiny mouth latched onto the breast—only to drift into oblivion. Melchior also thought of the time that he told his daughter to hold his hand as the two of them were walking in a busy market. His daughter proudly declared, "I can hold my own hand." Melchior again chuckled to himself, and a psalm then came to his mind: "like a child at rest is my soul within me." Like his circumstances which he could not control, all such memories came to him without any invitation on his part. No, he was not the captain of his own soul, but more like a stowaway who knew not where he was going but who wanted to journey. Being a wise man, he surmised that since he could neither control his circumstances nor his thoughts, perhaps he might use such interruptions to help him on his own journey. In this case, he said to himself that he ought to travel like a carefree child, never worrying about what the future may or may not hold.

At long last, Melchior arrived in Judea. He then made his way to Jerusalem, for he assumed that the promised peace-maker would come from a great city. When he inquired, however, about the whereabouts of the would-be deliverer, his queries were met with ridicule in that great city. Late one evening, and similar to the experience of Anchises, Melchior started to think that he had journeyed in vain; but he then watched a star fall from the sky and bury its brightness outside of that great city in an unassuming village called Bethlehem. Melchior knew that this was an omen, and that maybe the one that he longed to see was in Bethlehem. As he ventured to that village, he nevertheless second-guessed himself. "It would be most fitting," he mused, "for the prince of peace to come from the city of peace and not a backward village that is known only for its bread."

Consistent with such thinking, Melchior had hoped that he would miraculously find life when he saw the Christ child; but this did not happen. When others saw baby Jesus, they said there was nothing outstanding about him. He was just like other babies—burping, fussing, needing to be changed, and wanting human warmth. Similarly, nothing overtly miraculous ever happened as he watched baby Jesus grow into a child. Melchior mused to himself, *"he is only a child, a common child, a little boy from a poor family."*[8] It was just this commonness that proved to be miraculous, for Melchior slowly realized that the beauty of God comes in what is small, even helpless. "If," Melchior reasoned, "beauty comes to the world through innocence, then perhaps I myself should reflect more on simplicity and neediness."

An early test of Melchior's resolve came with Herod the Great. Like most despots, Herod was profoundly paranoid, such that he murdered anyone who might pose a threat to the story that he wanted to live (including members of his own family). It was out of such paranoia that Herod invited Melchior for dinner. While they were feasting, Herod asked Melchior information about the Christ child. Melchior made up righteous lies: he thought that Herod probably knew that the child was named Jesus and that the child lived in Bethlehem, so he told Herod that the parents of Jesus were named Mattathias and Abigail, and that they did not live in Bethlehem itself but in a hamlet outside of Bethlehem. Herod believed the story, which bought everyone the time needed to escape from Judea (Joseph, Mary, and Jesus went to Egypt; and Melchior himself returned to Persia). Herod then *slouched toward Bethlehem.*[9] Hoping that he might kill the promised messiah, and akin to murderous Pharaoh, he then ordered that every male child under the age of two be slaughtered; but, as Voldemort would experience, *the boy would not die.*[10] Herod justified this action by contending that the child was a threat to Roman rule (the truth, though, is that he fixated on himself, and nothing, not even children, was to get in the way of how his story ought to be fulfilled).

Vignette 4

John the Baptist

JOHN THE BAPTIST CLOAKED himself in animal skins, his long hair collected in matted knots, his grimy beard clung to his chicken-bone chest, and his eyes were piercing—as if he could see through a brick wall.

The Baptist might have been confused with a Cynic, for both his appearance and his message underlined the absurdity of society with all its silly pretenses about success. The fact, though, is that the Baptist was an uncompromising devotee of the Hebrew faith: he was particularly fond of those passages that concerned the end of the world; and he believed that he was the forerunner of the messiah through whom universal peace would come—but only after a bloody battle in Jerusalem.

While the Baptist told people to turn from godlessness, one would be mistaken in thinking that he was a killjoy ascetic. The righteousness that the Baptist preached involved the entire person: with regard to outward righteousness, to Herod he said, "stop your sexual relationship with your brother's sister"; as for inner righteousness, to those who trusted in themselves he said that all are equally needy. The righteousness that the Baptist proclaimed was also costly, for it presupposed death to selfishness—when people asked what they must do, the Baptist answered that they needed to live for others: "the one with extra clothes must share with him who has none, and the one who has food must do the same."

One must not think that the Baptist had it all together, though, for he did have his demons—the chief of which was his relationship with his father, Zechariah. The Baptist had learned to be combative from Zechariah, who complemented his idealism with ferocious arguments. (One temple priest sanctioned Zechariah by saying, "You are a priest. People come to you for your prayers, to be forgiven, and to learn the way of God. They don't come to you to argue.")

The argumentative and idealistic nature of the Baptist followed him when he left home and became a traveling preacher. On different occasions, for instance, the Baptist had "discussions" about alcohol. Some cited the Mosaic command that people should drink "wine and strong drink" as they worship with joy in the temple. Others protested, citing Solomon who said "wine is a mocker, strong drink is a brawler, whoever is led astray by them is not wise." The Baptist himself ascribed to the latter view. In secret, however, and while dwelling on his broken relationship with his father, he drank. At the beginning, this was no problem; but as time wore on, the drinking started to control him—even exacerbating his problem with Zechariah. The Baptist then told himself to repent of drinking, but this inner-proclamation proved to be as impotent and empty as the wine-skin that he both hated and loved. No doubt, his preaching was still like a raging storm, but the eye of that storm had ceased to be still, for the Baptist was no longer self-confident.

Perhaps starting with his awareness that alcohol had a grip on him, the Baptist then became aware of a shadow that lurked behind his ability to identify sin. "It is almost," he thought, "that I enjoy pointing out the sin of others. What is more, *I think that I protest too much*, for the very things that I rail against in others are things that I struggle with in my own life."[11] The shadow came into the light when God-fearing people asked the Baptist what they should do. When the Baptist said that they should "repent," the word sounded hollow. ("What," the Baptist asked himself, "do they need to repent of?") All the same, he felt guilty if he did not use the word. The Baptist started to think that maybe he did not understand repentance. He therefore looked again at the Isaiah scroll. In it he read that salvation expresses itself "in repentance and rest." While the Baptist thought that he understood "repentance," the "rest" part of the equation eluded him. The Baptist then had a gloomy thought: "maybe," he surmised, "I need to repent of my repentance."

It is profoundly difficult to criticize something that one holds to dearly. So it was with the Baptist: repenting of his understanding of repentance amounted to a paradigm shift, a complete re-thinking of what God wants—and even who God is. As difficult as the task was, humility put the Baptist in a good place. "The messiah," he had said, "must become greater, and I must become less." This emphasis on humility was similarly implicit in his use of Isaiah: "A voice of one calling in the desert: 'Prepare the way of the Lord. Make straight in the desert a highway for our God. Every valley shall be exalted, and every mountain shall be made low. The rough ground shall become smooth, and the rugged places a plain.'" Such language was at one time used with reference to a visit of an important official. In preparation for such a visit, people fixed and leveled the roadways. The Baptist, however, had understood this language figuratively: humility is the basis, bar none, of welcoming the kingdom of the messiah into one's life. The Baptist had hitherto known about humility but he only knew humility when he was confronted by his own brokenness, by being weak and needy—all of which made him *absolutely dependent* on God.[12]

Much earlier, the Baptist had equated humility with loathing oneself, a self-deprecatory worm theology. As he grew in his understanding of humility, however, the Baptist understood humility as the recognition that everything that is good about oneself comes from God. So also, he learned that repentance is not just a matter of turning away from what is sinful. The Baptist was fond of saying that the believer defeats sin not by running from it, but by running to God. (Being the extreme person that he was, the Baptist similarly said that it is idolatrous to turn to goodness rather than to the ground of all goodness, God himself.) It was out of such humility that the Baptist could confess (in the words of his favorite prophet), "in the past he humbled me, but on those living in the land of the shadow of death a light has dawned."

Vignette 5

Joseph and Mary, the Parents of Jesus

WHILE JESUS ENJOYED PLAYING with Joseph, his fondest memories were in the carpenter shop, for it was there that the two had bonded.

Jesus remembered when Joseph had carelessly cut a board. Jesus said that Joseph did not cut it too short; rather, his father had not made the line wide enough! The two of them laughed hysterically at this. Joseph then started to measure another board, but Jesus suggested that Joseph remeasure the first board. To Joseph's surprise, the board was the correct length after all. (Years later, when Joseph learned that Jesus performed miracles, he said that perhaps Jesus had stretched the board.)

While Jesus was like other boys, he had a particular fascination with God.

On one spring evening, the local rabbi came for his annual visit. At the close of the visit, the conversation moved to faithfulness.

The rabbi said, "We must keep the statutes of Moses and learn the teachings of the elders. Doing so includes weekly attendance at my service, for I am the only person in the community who can read." Joseph, who was a pillar both in the community and the synagogue, nodded in agreement; but the non-verbal cues of young Jesus were not so positive—such that the rabbi became disgruntled. Wanting to elicit a response, the rabbi explicitly asked adolescent Jesus what he thought. Jesus said, "It seems to me that you are more concerned with people coming to your service than you are with people themselves. What is more important, that people love God, or that they go to your synagogue services?" The rabbi was miffed by such precociousness. As for Joseph, he was not upset with what Jesus had said, only that he dared to say it.

Mary also knew that there was something different about Jesus.

Every year the family journeyed from Nazareth to celebrate the Passover in Jerusalem. On one such occasion, Jesus found himself in the temple precincts chatting with one of the priests. Jesus had become so engrossed in the conversation that he had forgotten the time. When at long last Jesus joined his family to go back to Nazareth, Mary asked him why he was late.

"I am sorry, mom. It is not every day that I meet temple priests, so I guess that I got caught up in the moment. I was having a wonderful discussion with a priest about the need to worship. I happily agreed that all humanity is born to worship, but our conversation turned sour when I suggested that worship in the temple might repel people. The reason that I gave was that people might confuse hypocrisy with the goodness of our Father. I was not at all suggesting that the priest himself was one such hypocrite. On the contrary! He seemed to be both devout and kind. Perhaps, however, I was naive, for the priest was offended—even calling me arrogant and saying that I needed to mind my place. The priest said to me, 'The acne on your pocked face may well be caused by the same demon that makes you challenge what is holy.' That's how our conversation ended, for I did not know how to continue without making the priest yet more angry."

Mary noticed that there had been change in the thinking of Jesus: where years earlier Jesus spoke of "God," he now spoke of God as "Father." Mary knew that there was nothing disingenuous about this: Jesus simply called God "Father"—even the way that a son might refer to his daddy. (Much can be learned from the designation "Father." The notions that God is aloof, unconcerned, or unapproachable are altogether unlike the faith of Jesus—for whom everything was immediate. Like God the Father, the past and the future are here, now—such that a historian, a philosopher, a singer, or a religious teacher might unconsciously tap into universal thought.)

Vignette 6

Hezekiah, the Essene

LIKE OTHER GROUPS THAT are more concerned with conformity than unity, there were disagreements among the Essenes. One such disagreement was between the Baptist and Hezekiah.

Hezekiah upbraided the Baptist: "The pre-condition of being baptized should be conformity to the faith of our fathers. As it is, you simply tell people to be good. To the Roman soldier you say, 'Don't be needlessly violent'; and to the Jewish tax collector you say, 'Don't take too much money from people.' You ought to tell the Roman soldier to turn from his paganism, and you ought to tell the tax collector to cease taking Jewish money to support Rome."

John responded with thoughtful anger: "Faith expresses itself in justice and mercy. The soldier, gentile though he may be, can find truth within himself, for the God of Moses has put his truth into every heart. I don't only want people to become devout Jews; I am also calling them to be consistent with the truth that they know."

What John had said was outside the confines of Hezekiah's belief system (make no mistake, it was a system—unyielding as the grave and as lifeless as its corpse). But Hezekiah refused to be outdone, for getting bettered signaled weakness.

Hezekiah, who thought that he must be right because John was so wrong, continued. "Another problem that I have with your baptism is that you encourage people to follow Jesus. While devout Jews adhere to worship in the temple, the very abode of God, Jesus said that he is greater than the temple—as if God resided in him. Consistent with such blasphemy, you said that you are not worthy to untie his sandals, and you addressed him as 'the lamb of God that takes away the sin of the world.'"

Not waiting for a response, Hezekiah carried on: "Your aspirations are also selfish, for Jesus is your cousin. This deceiver has fed your ego, for he said that you are the greatest prophet who has ever lived."

Hezekiah, who by this time was losing his breath, then concluded his rant: "I advise you to turn from your stupidity. You are undermining the true faith and stirring up the ire of Herod—and his vengeance will be swift."

Hezekiah, John thought, was like concrete—all mixed up and permanently set in his ways. Because John had learned that arguing is a waste of breath when someone's mind is fixed, he said nothing more.

Vignette 7

The Serpent

LIKE THE SON OF Man, I had modest beginnings. I was just a snake that loved to bask on warm rocks. Life was easy for me. After gorging myself on a frog, I would spend the next few days digesting it. I also spent my time lollygagging about the garden: swimming in pools, slithering under shade trees, and vexing silly sparrows.

The Lord God had made me the shrewdest of all animals, and everyone in the garden knew it. I was even more clever than the man (who, after all, was made from clay). As for the woman, she was even more gullible than the frogs that I consumed. (*I'll be damned if I can recall their names.*)[13]

Everything was wonderful until the Lord God, who then became my Adversary (the Hebrew of which is "satan"), drove the couple from the garden. The Adversary was himself somewhat of a dullard, not nearly as clever as me, for he had to ask questions: to the man, he asked, "where are you?"; he also had to ask the woman, "what is this that you have done?" (People have angst about suffering; my existential concern is how such a dolt could get a lofty position.)

In an act of reckless stupidity, the Adversary then cast the couple from the garden. With this intolerable action, all that was wonderful became sordid—my days of leisure had come to a pitiable end. (I could never return to the garden, for, in her rage at losing her home, the woman seized some of the fire that her deceptive cousin Prometheus had stolen, and she engulfed the garden in flames with it.)

My evolution from simple snake to prince of darkness developed over many centuries. This evolution has been both a blessing and a curse (if I may use such language). It has been a blessing insofar as I have taken on a godlike status: no longer was I a simple reptile, for silly people thought that I was all-knowing and everywhere. With my evolution came names. I despise the name "Beelzebub" (for I don't only have dominion over flies). A better name, I thought, is that of "Lucifer." I like this name, both because it arose from a fraudulent understanding of a scripture (I love to twist sacred words), and because it was first used with reference to that planet that brings light to the world (thus undermining the blasphemous association that people make between me and darkness). Being what they are, people also gave me a number, 666. But a curse resided in these blessings. I am blamed for every evil action: "the devil made me do it" is the repugnant refrain that makes every nerve along my spine tingle. Such language compels me to strike the heels of every member of humanity.

Individuals blame me rather than themselves. The woman's answer to the Adversary is typical: when the Adversary asked her, "What is this that you have done?" the woman said, "the serpent deceived me and I ate." As it was then, throughout all time humanity has played this blame game. This game is delightfully venomous when a collective is blamed. A state only apologizes for having done wrong long after it has been unjust. It is, similarly, darkly comical when the church is to blame: churchmen then scramble to contain hypocrisy—lest all hell break loose. Adding to the comedy is that those who contained the hypocrisy are then granted more power—the very thing that led to the initial hypocrisy.

Closely related to blame is the projection of faults. I was delighted to see this in the man: when the Adversary asked him, "did you eat from the tree?" the man replied, "the woman you made for me gave me some of the fruit to eat." Here we see that the man cleverly shifted the blame away from himself both to the woman and, in an aggressively passive manner, to the Adversary himself. Such shifting away from oneself is how projection manifests itself. I myself only exist as a projection of humanity (yet, in order to justify themselves, if I was only *a hypothesis* people would *invent* me).[14]

Whether it is blame or projection, then, what we see in the garden is true of all history—it's as if the garden is a prototype. Starting with deceit in the garden, *history is just one damned thing after another.*[15] This would all be fine (for I love enmity), but the only problem is that I am accused: "the devil made me do it," they say. Give your heads a shake, people! Don't accuse me for the violence on which you yourselves gorge! I am flawless, and you are flawed—like the innocent goat upon which the Hebrews placed their sin and drove into the solitary wilderness.

Does not scripture command you not to slander? Does not scripture exhort you to refrain from judging others? You have both slandered and judged me. But cunning creature that I am, I will continue to use your own wickedness against you—for so long as you blame and project, mayhem and strife will abound.

I must here ask, "Why do people hate to accept blame?" The answer is simple. Like the Adversary, they are full of pride, which I hate and love all at once: I hate the pride of humanity because I alone deserve first place; but I love pride, this *anti-God begetting of all sin*, because I use it in clever ways.[16]

In their pride, people live as though all that exists is about them, that each one is the Adversary's gift to humanity. Every individual chooses to think of themselves as royalty. As such, they *would rather reign in hell than serve in heaven*.[17] Everyone is also a hero of their own story. "If only," they say, "others were like me." Each regards himself as unique (but, even as Barenaked Ladies will say, "*it's all been done before*"—the thoughts and abilities of any one "stellar" individual have hundreds of iterations through history).[18] It is not a question of adoration. People may even hate themselves (and they would be right to do so, vile creatures that they are), but it is only self that has permission to loathe self. No one else can do so—not even the Adversary.

I am proud of the subtle way in which I used pride in the garden. When I first spoke to the woman, I said, "Did God really say, 'You must not eat from any tree in the garden?'" By using the word "really," I created doubt in her mind. My use of "any tree" complemented such doubt, for I knew that she would correct me—and to my infernal delight I was right, for the woman then said, "God said, 'You must not touch the tree in the middle of the garden.'" She was following my scheme perfectly, for the Adversary had said nothing about touching the tree. Because the woman loved herself, she then stepped into my cunning trap and ate from the tree.

I used a similar strategy with the Son of Man. I tempted him with wealth, with power, and with prestige; but unlike the first man, the Son of Man had grounded himself in the lies of the Adversary—such that I could not beguile him. I even tried to quote his scriptures to misdirect him, but nothing worked. I had failed, but I knew that the time would come when I would succeed. "The Son of Man may be loyal to the Adversary," I reasoned, "but loyal to a fault—for people are loyal only to themselves."

Because I have a record of twisting what the Adversary says, some people have blasphemously referred to me as "the father of lies." Even my friend Death slandered me: "you've been lying so long that you don't know what is real." Such accusations are as uncharitable as they are untrue. What, after all, is truth? I am reminded of an episode from Crete. When various people denied that Zeus was immortal, Epimenides the Cretan said, "Cretans are always liars." How should one believe Epimenides? Epimenides from Crete was truthfully lying when he said that all Cretans are liars. (The god-like Muses who inspired Hesiod also know how to spin lies into truth; and the goddess named Rumour similarly mingles fact and fiction.) As for my own ability to mix truth and lies, it is altogether natural, for my tongue is forked. I should, therefore, not be blamed, for a fellow cannot be blamed for having been created in a certain way. If I truly tell lies, it is the Adversary's fault. Indeed, I should be praised rather than slandered, for *truth would not be the same without the lies that I have made up*.[19]

(I predict that a time will come when, like me, people will contend that truth and lies do not exist. Rather than saying, "absolutes may exist but I don't know them," they will come to the absurd conclusion that absolutely no absolutes exist. I will then jeer, for the scheming that I used in the garden will once again prove itself.)

Like my blend of truth and lies, the Adversary tried to mix things when he made man: he thought that by breathing his spirit into the clay image humanity would become a life-giving mixture of heaven and earth. But unlike my successful inter-mixture of truth and lies, the Adversary failed miserably—for the clay image only loved itself. The Adversary is like my servant Pygmalion, who naively thought that his sculpture could become a beautiful woman. No doubt, the statue became alive as he kissed it, but its heart was as lifeless as stone. The Adversary may also be likened to a desperate alchemist who vainly tries to mix substances to produce gold— the result is a blend that is worthy only of the dung heap. The Adversary has learned that people are neither heavenly nor earthly, but a worthless admixture of the two—like a double-minded man who says to himself, "I know what I ought to do, but I can't do it."

I must be wary, however, for this mixture of heaven and earth is very powerful when it recognizes just how weak it is. The ones I fear the most are those who ask, "what do I have that I did not receive?" Like the Adversary, the Son of Man may encourage humanity to unite heaven and earth in their lives; but I will thwart his plans, for, like his Father, he will not create beauty out of ugliness.

Vignette 8

Akiva, the Scribe

I AM A "SOPHER"—ONE who counts the letters of holy scripture.

It is an honor to copy Torah, but I must be attentive. In addition to having superb orthographic skills, I must be careful to keep the rules of my trade. At my best, I can copy four words per minute; but as the day dims, I must slow down to two or three words—for being hasty, and therefore making a mistake, is a great sin.

A common sin includes copying the same thing twice. A good example of this appears in the Tower of Babel story. Three times we there read that people "were scattered over the face of all the earth." Because of this repetition, some scribes have copied it too many times, or they have omitted it where they should have copied it. Like the story itself, such scribes have been "confused."

A chief safeguard to keep me from sinning is mindless counting.

The middle letter of the Torah is the letter "vav" of the word "belly" (close to the middle of Leviticus). There are 304, 805 letters in Torah, so it is just a matter of dividing this sum by two and counting from the beginning or from the end. (I bow before this letter, which, by itself, often means "and.") The middle words, "darosh darash" ("diligently inquire"), are also close to the middle of Leviticus. As with the middle letter of Torah, it is just a matter of counting the words to ensure that "darosh darash" is indeed the dead center. If either the middle letter or the middle words are not correct, a grievous error has been made.

Torah is my favorite section of scripture to copy, and Genesis is my favorite in the Torah, and the early stories of Genesis are my favorite within these favorites.

I am particularly fascinated by the plethora of word-plays. Adam, for example, whose name means humanity, was created from "adamah," which means dirt—even as "woman" (ishah) was made from "man" (iysh). Similarly, at the end of the garden story both man and woman were "naked" (arummim) only to read in the next sentence that the serpent was "cunning" (arum)—such cunning would expose their nakedness.

I am also fascinated by numerology in the early stories of Genesis. I note, for example, that fifty letters after the first "taw" is the letter "vav," and fifty letters later is the letter "resh," and fifty letters later is the letter "heh"—which together spells "Torah." I am similarly struck by the preponderance of the number seven in the creation story: there are seven days, "God" is mentioned twenty-one times, and the first sentence has twenty-eight letters (both of which are divisible by seven). Given that the number seven is symbolic of divine perfection, this should occasion no surprise. The significance of numbers may also be seen in the fact that Enoch lived for three hundred and sixty-five years, which corresponds to the number of days in a solar year. (It is no wonder that he did not die, for he was complete!) So also, one can reflect on the age of Methuselah. We often associate longevity with righteousness, but aged Methuselah challenges this assumption—for the nine hundred and sixty-ninth year of Methuselah was the six hundredth year of Noah, which is when the flood happened. (The conclusion is inescapable: Methuselah perished with the wicked.)

The number forty also intrigues me. This is the number of testing and trial: it rained for forty days and nights; Moses was on Sinai for forty days; Israel was in the wilderness for forty years (one year for each of the forty days that the spies looked at Canaan); Elijah, who was also in the wilderness, fled from Jezebel for forty days; and Nineveh repented for forty days. One should not be surprised, then, that stories concerning testing and trial should be divisible by forty.

Another story that is divisible by 40 is, again, the story of Babel. While the story as we have it consists of 121 words, in its original (and therefore perfect) form it was probably 120 words—for 120 is divisible by three (unlike scribes, Hashem makes no mistakes). This story concerns humanity's overweening pride. The irony in this story is that whereas the people sought to ascend to God by building a tower, Hashem had "to go down to see" what the people were doing. This irony is accentuated by a delightful pun: the people "built" (laban) a tower, and Hashem (inverting the very word that the people used) "confused" (nabal) them.

(This story is not unlike Ovid's tale in which giants placed mountains on top of other mountains to reach to the heavens. Ovid's tale, however, is just a myth. It also lacks the irony that Hashem had to come down, which does not surprise me for Mount Sinai eclipses Mount Olympus. Maybe, though I am wrong. Maybe the tale is from Hesiod, not Ovid. Hesiod was supposedly a divinely inspired shepherd boy—but we know that only one shepherd boy was ever inspired by Hashem. It doesn't matter whether it was Ovid, or Hesiod, for ever since my boyhood, I have been taught that how one grows up shapes one's faith, such that I can scarcely blame pagans for believing wrong things.)

Whereas the Babel story is all about humanity's confusion, the following story concerns the call of Abraham (whose numerical equivalence is 41). This story is the reciprocal of the Tower of Babel story: whereas the arrogant builders of the tower sought to make a "name" (shem) for themselves by building to the heavens, Hashem said that he would make the "name" (shem) of Abraham great—because he left everything to follow Hashem. Similarly, prior to the call of Abraham, one reads of a "curse" five times, but in the call of Abraham itself one reads of a "blessing" five times. The curse that humanity brought on itself will thus be undone by Hashem's five-fold blessing: all humanity will be blessed through the offspring of Abraham, the Son of Man, who is also referred to as the Son of David. (The numerical equivalence of "David" is 14, so a story about the Son of David should be a multiple of 14—like 42, which is just beyond the numerical equivalence of "Abraham.")

I could go on and on to discuss the numeric significance of other names, many other word-plays, the meaning behind "misspelled" words, and other features of the eternal Torah, but doing so would keep me from studying more of Torah myself; and I must not be distracted by people, for it is the sacred text and its inerrant teachings that demand my attention.

(Last week a little boy came to my porch to play with my daughter. I told him that she had gone with my wife. As he waited for them to return, the boy occupied himself with humming, which bothered me, and so I commanded him to stop. This worked for a few minutes, but the boy then resumed his humming. I became angry and yelled at him. Tears welled-up in his eyes as he left the porch, but he stubbornly stuck around in the yard and kicked stones. I was then compelled to leave my study of that verse that teaches that boys who curse their fathers are to be put to death. I ran at the boy, and I smote him. It would be, I think, better for people to jump into the ocean with a millstone around their necks than to disturb the study of Torah.)

The messianic pretender from Galilee teaches that concentration on the text produces a loveless and bookish faith. It seems to me that this heretic wants to have his cake and eat it too. On the one hand, he says that every "jot" (by which he must mean the letter "yod," the most common letter in the Torah, which appears 31,530 times) and every "tittle" (by which he must mean the letter "tet," the least common letter in the Torah, which appears 1,820 times) of the Torah is from Hashem. This is consistent with the faith. On the other hand, however, he says that every "jot" and "tittle" find their fulfillment in him—a blasphemy worthy of forty lashes! As with the copying of the tower story, the messianic pretender is confused. If people simply learned to place their hopes on the written text and its heavenly truths, such people would have life—for "by the word of the Lord, the heavens were made." It is the letter, not the spirit, that gives life.

Vignette 9

Benjamin, the Politician

Lᴇsᴛ Jᴜᴅᴇᴀ ᴜɴɴᴇᴄᴇssᴀʀɪʟʏ ᴘʀᴏᴠᴏᴋᴇ Rome, my God-given role as a member of the Sanhedrin is to understand political and religious persuasions.

I have learned that Pilate is religiously ambivalent. While Pilate presents himself as a devotee of imperial gods, he only does so for persona reasons—but, as he himself told me, his religion is to please Rome. Not unlike Pilate, Herod is more concerned with maintaining his power than worship of any god. Pilate and Herod are game changers in Judea; but I would be unfaithful to my calling if I did not also strive to understand smaller players. Such players often have exalted understandings of themselves—they think that they are somehow extraordinary or even, in some cases, central to world history.

Jesus of Nazareth is one such player. The danger of Jesus is tied to how he challenges views of scripture and tradition.

Like others, Jesus believes that the Hebrew scriptures are true. I doubt that he thinks that all the stories in the scriptures really happened as one reads them—talking snakes and donkeys and the like. (Jesus might say, "The stories in scripture are altogether true, but they did not all happen.") This view angers the religious authorities, for such leaders have reasoned that knowing what their god wants is straightforward: if the will of their god is housed in scriptures, then it is simply a matter of consulting the scriptures. (This is really not much different than how someone might study the entrails of an animal to divine the will of the gods.)

A common understanding views scripture as a universe unto itself. Where sentences in scripture raise questions that they themselves do not answer, scribes interpret them by means of other sentences. A question might be asked, for example, about why the raven hovered above the ark and refused to fly away. It did so, so this reasoning would have it, because the raven thought that Noah had sexual designs on its mate (the preceding story concerns sexual relations between different species—angels and humans).

Contrary to this idea that scripture should be interpreted by scripture, Jesus believes that scripture is to be interpreted through humanity. People, he would say, are more important than a book. On one occasion, one of my spies told me how an Essene bragged that he was so zealous in keeping the Sabbath day that he fought against having a bowel movement on it. Jesus told the Essene that this assumes that the Sabbath is more important than people. "The important thing is to live in the Sabbath every day," Jesus said. Not surprisingly, the Essene asked for justification for this view from scripture. "Whereas," Jesus said, "there was 'evening and morning' on the first six days of creation, the story does not mention 'evening and morning' on the Sabbath. To those in the kingdom, every moment is Sabbath."

Let me now turn to the understanding that Jesus has of tradition. Just as Jesus says that scripture is to be interpreted through humanity, so he says that the tradition of the elders is to be interpreted through humanity.

The tradition of the elders is regarded as a "fence" around scripture: if, so the reasoning goes, one keeps this tradition, then one will be faithful. Keeping the Sabbath day holy means not working on it; but what constitutes work? Walking too far would be work, so the tradition of the elders includes how far one can walk on a Sabbath. Spitting also constitutes work, for if saliva happens to fall on a seed that seed might germinate—which would amount to the work of planting.

One problem of the tradition of the elders, according to Jesus, is that it has nothing to say about the heart. One of my spies told me that a rather somber-looking seminarian asked Jesus, "Why do your disciples break the tradition of the elders by not washing their hands before they eat?" (One can become "unclean" by such actions as touching a dead body, sitting on a seat that a woman having her period has sat on, or, as in this case, by not washing one's hands.) Jesus, who seems to have an uncanny ability to know what people are about even before they speak, knew that the seminarian wanted to be proper. Jesus jolted the seminarian with a vulgar, although humorous, analogy: "eating food with unwashed hands does not make one unclean; but the waste that comes out of a person can make one unclean."

The spy told me that while people who were gathered smirked at the analogy, the seminarian failed to see any humour—distraught as he was by its crudity. Jesus then continued: "It is not outward obedience that impresses God. What God wants is inward cleanliness—a heartfelt mercy toward others."

Many people in Judea think that the scriptures and the traditions are a "yoke" that unites them to God. No doubt, the yoke is heavy, and one must almost cease being human to carry it; but better a wooden yoke, than a wooden cross—which Jesus might be crucified upon if he continues to preach that his yoke is easy to bear and that his teachings are altogether human. If, indeed, Jesus is crucified, I will be content: my calling is to keep relations with Judea and Rome peaceable.

Vignette 10

Maccabeus, the Zealot

A Zealot named Maccabeus was drunk at an inn.

"While it is true," Maccabeus slurred, "that the messiah will in some sense be divine, the messianic pretender from Galilee is not divine, and folks have no reason for thinking that he is the messiah. When the messiah comes, he will slaughter the gentile oppressors. I don't know just how he will do this. Maybe, like Moses of old, before he crosses the Jordan he will drown the unbelievers in its blood; maybe, like the prophet Amos, he will call fire down from heaven to consume them. I don't know how the messiah will save us, but he will do so. Has this Jesus done any such thing?"

"Jesus is common, even boring. Contrary to being violent, he advocates that we should forgive the Romans and that we should pray for them, and that this is the only way toward peace. *'Peace?': I hate the word, as I hate Hades.*"[20]

Maccabeus paused to burp before continuing.

"Did the Romans ever show mercy to us? They want to rule over us at any cost. Their so-called peace is based on our blood: if we don't fall in line with them, they will kill us. Let us be killed, then! We must never submit to them."

"What, then, about this Jesus?"

The inn-keeper, who, like the ferryman over Styx, had a mass of unkempt white hair straggling from his chin and a dirty garment hanging from his stooped shoulders, agreed with Maccabeus. "Let us drink to the man speaking truth about the renegade," the inn-keeper said. "Years ago, I sent away a pregnant woman with her husband. I told them that they might find room in a barn—that is, if the animals had room for dirty vagabonds. I would do the same to Jesus, for I have *no time for losers*.[21] Those who hail Jesus as the Son of Man *are bloody, ignorant, apes*.[22] As Seneca (that sober-minded Roman) said, "the difference between ignorant people and a drunkard is that whereas a drunkard may turn from his drink, an ignorant person will not turn from ignorance."

A brother of a disciple of Jesus carefully observed Maccabeus and the inn-keeper belching and pontificating. He himself nodded in agreement.

Feeling encouraged both by the inn-keeper and the disciple's brother, Maccabeus continued: "While Jesus avoids identifying himself, his words tell us what he really thinks. Before he healed an invalid, he said that he 'forgave' him for his sin. My complaint is not that he healed the invalid, but that he had the audacity to say 'I forgive you.' What blasphemous nonsense! Is he God? On another occasion, Jesus and his disciples were caught eating grain from their stalks on the Sabbath. I don't care at all about how such work desecrates the Sabbath. My complaint is that Jesus then said, 'I am the Lord of the Sabbath.' This Jesus fellow thinks that he is one with the Almighty—but he is only like the big guy in the sky insofar as, like him, he has no concern with the plight of his people. (Jesus reminds me of that famed astronomer who, because he was gazing at the heavens, fell into a pit.) If Jesus was any earthly good, he would wreak the vengeance of the Almighty One on our godless foes."

"Inn-keeper, fetch me another drink! *I thirst*."[23]

Because the speech of Maccabeus was becoming incomprehensible, the brother of the disciple thought that it was an opportune time to enter the conversation. "According to my brother, who, I am ashamed to say, has been following Jesus, Jesus avoids calling himself the messiah because he thinks that people might misunderstand him. The title that Jesus prefers to use is 'Son of Man.' Neither my brother nor I know what this title means." Inebriated Maccabeus responded with, "Who the hell cares who Jesus is? All that I know is that he is not the messiah, and those who think that he is ought to have their heads examined—that is, unless the Romans don't decapitate them first." At this, the tangled conversation ended, for the laughter was uproarious.

Vignette 11

Simon the Cynic, and Hermogenes

AT THE SAME TIME that the conversation between the Zealot and Malchus was taking place, Simon, who was a cobbler from Gadara, spoke to his friend Hermogenes. (Simon and Hermogenes were friends, but they had little in common: Simon had disregard for the trappings of society, while Hermogenes was very successful.)

Because various teachings of Jesus accorded with the teachings of Cynicism (even Gadara's own Menippus), Simon asked Hermogenes if he had heard about Jesus from Nazareth. Hermogenes reticently nodded in the affirmative.

Simon then said, "I am enthralled with what Jesus teaches. The trouble that I am having in understanding Jesus pertains to his belief in the Hebrew God. I have learned to replace his ideas about God with concepts that I find more palatable. When Jesus uses the word 'Father,' I understand him to mean 'the logic of the cosmos' (perhaps akin to what some followers of Pythagoras have thought of numbers—certain and trustworthy, yet cold and removed)."

As Simon carried on, he pretended not to notice the discomfort of Hermogenes. "My understanding of the teachings of Jesus can only develop as I learn more about where he gets his ideas. I have tried reading the Jewish scriptures, but they are impractical. It seems to me that they teach different things about virtue: whereas the laws of Moses teach that virtue is tied to doing or not doing this or that, other scriptures teach that virtue expresses itself in trusting the Jewish God. I think that the matter is simpler: virtue is found in an untainted heart. All the same, I do have appreciation for some of the prophets in those scriptures, for their messages were accompanied with strange actions: Isaiah walked around naked for three years; Ezekiel cooked food with human excrement; and Hosea married a prostitute. (Such actions remind me of Diogenes, who slept in a tub in the streets of Athens to underline the absurdity of human values.) People need to be awakened from the slumber that society has brought upon them; and such awakening may take on unacceptable forms."

Perhaps because Hermogenes had heard this all before, he sat expressionless before Simon. This continuous disregard angered Simon, such that he became personal. "The Nazarene was right," said Simon, "when he said that 'a man may lose his soul in the process of trying to gain the world.' You say that I am an underachiever because I repair shoes when I could be great; but at least my soul is intact. I fear for you, for while you strive to excel in this world, you don't seem to care about goodness."

When Hermogenes finally spoke, he stammered—which is what he did when concepts would not seem to do justice to what was in his heart. "Yes, I agree with the statutes of Cynicism . . . er . . . I agree that I may have been duped by the empty aspirations of the world . . . um . . . Is this what you have wanted . . . uh . . . to hear me say? But your judgment is superficial . . . er . . . It only looks at what I do, not my intentions. Cynicism has not taught you about your heart. "

At this stammering rebuke of Hermogenes, Simon became uncharacteristically sullen. The chastisement came at an inopportune time, for Simon's cobbling business was not bringing in enough money, and his health was failing. As with other things in life that were *falling apart*, Cynicism itself had become flawed in a fundamental way—for it did not address purity of heart.[24]

As the months passed, Simon's condition worsened. There did not seem to be anything that anyone could do or say to rescue Simon from his depression. Like other unfortunate people, Simon eventually became homeless, and then driven out to the countryside. While there in isolation, his condition morphed into madness—such that, among other things, he cut himself with stones.

Boys would sometimes go to the Gadarene countryside to vex Simon: they threw stones at him and demolished his make-shift shelters. They also called him names, the favourite of which was "Legion"—for it seemed that denizens of evil spirits inhabited him. (Simon often said, "*there's someone in my head but it's not me.*")[25]

Things began to change for the better, though, through two people. The first person was one of the boys, whose name was (oddly enough) *Muishkin*.[26] While at first Muishkin stood by as the other boys taunted Simon, he started to view Simon with pity. Muishkin then actively defended Simon by telling the boys not to be so harsh, and he finally came to Simon's defence by throwing clods of clay at the boys who were hurling stones at Simon. What happened next was beautiful. Following Muishkin's lead, other boys became attached to Simon—sometimes they shared treats with him that they had stolen from the market, and at other times they helped Simon build a shelter. This new treatment gave Simon something that he had never known: acceptance.

The second person who helped Simon was Jesus. When Jesus was passing through the area, he stopped to talk to Simon. Jesus taught Simon that a good disciple is not simply one who does the right things, but someone who also grows in purity of heart—someone who thinks the best of others, who prefers others to himself, who forgives others, who, in a word, loves others.

Vignette 12

Two Disciples of John the Baptist

A YOUNG DISCIPLE OF John the Baptist was both confused and indignant when he learned of the imprisonment of John:

"John was right in asserting that people must repent before they follow the messiah, and he was right in saying that the messiah would defeat the enemies of Judea—but he was wrong in identifying Jesus as the messiah. John was, himself, not clear about precisely how Jesus was the messiah. He even sent me to inquire if Jesus really was the messiah. Within John's question, 'Who are you, Jesus?' is the complete undermining of John. I should have known much earlier that behind all John's blusterings there lurked uncertainty."

One of the leaders of the disciples of John was equally abject over the imprisonment of John, but his reaction was more nuanced:

"Idealistic minds often suppose that truth must accord with their blacks and whites; but while truth is pure, it is rarely simple. Like John, I am puzzled over the identity of Jesus. John wondered whether Jesus was the messiah, and so he sent me to ask Jesus. The answer that Jesus gave was typical, for it only raised more questions. Perhaps (and I am thinking out loud), Jesus thought that John's understanding of the messiah was too limited, and so his response was intentionally ambiguous. I just don't know what to think; but maybe what is most important is not believing in a particular way, but believing that God will surprise us. When we look at the history of how God has worked, he always surprised his people. Why should it be any different with the messiah? If such is the case, John is not to be blamed for his ignorance—for his honest ignorance amounts to faith:

John did not know who Jesus was, but he did know that God was somehow working through Jesus."

The young disciple remained unconvinced. In his mind, both John and the leader had compromised in different ways: John did so by confessing his ignorance; and the leader did so by saying that faith includes accepting what is ambiguous.

Vignette 13

The Samaritan Woman

"When will your husband return?" the judge asked as he disrobed me. Before I could answer, the door burst open and several men started to drag me outside—but the judge nervously escaped the scene.

I complained, saying to the men who were yanking me by the hair, "At least let me cover myself with this blanket." The men consented (if they brought me out naked it would have created scandal). I then wrapped the blanket around myself, but because it was small it did not cover me entirely—one breast remained exposed.

(The men could have seized me anytime, but, they thought, the fact that Jesus was near made the timing fortuitous—as if Fate was smiling upon them.)

The men then threw me to the street, as they might toss a rotting carcass. They did so awkwardly—lest by touching sin they themselves become sin. The men then summoned Jesus. They devoutly asked Jesus, "We just caught this woman being unfaithful. Moses told us to stone such women. What do you think?"

"Yes, by all means," Jesus said. "Let her be stoned."

At this, I was horrified, and the men were flustered. We were both bewildered when Jesus then stooped down and wrote in the dirt. I don't think that most of the onlookers knew what he was writing, for they were illiterate. The men, however, knew full well. Whatever it was, it made them uncomfortable. Perhaps he etched the names of the women they had ogled. I don't know.

Jesus then arose and said, "Let the man who has no sin start the stoning."

At this, the men looked down and slowly left—as if they themselves had become disrobed (while they loved being judges, they left the court-room when their thoughts had become visible).

While I was most relieved, I did not allow my deliverance to obscure my belief. Jesus was a Jew, and only Samaritans believe the right things; but I was puzzled. "How," I asked myself, "could a Jew be good?" I then challenged Jesus. I confronted him with different matters, the chief of which concerned the revelation of God to Moses on Mount Gerizim—not Mount Sinai, as Jews wrongly believe; but Jesus did not address my queries.

Jesus only seemed to hear questions that mattered—as if too much questioning annoyed him.[27] Jesus then asked a question that matters: "Do you think that you can be faithful to God if you are not faithful to others?" As he asked this, he knew my heart—*it seemed like he knew me, for he looked right through me.*[28] I knew then that there was something special about him. That same day I introduced my friends to Jesus. I said to them, "*Here is the man who is the answer that makes my questions disappear.*"[29]

Like I had done, my friends then accosted Jesus with volleys of questions (they wanted to see if he was on the right side). Rather than answering the questions, Jesus said that loving Truth includes the silencing of unhelpful questions.

(I have since concluded that the common view that there is no such thing as a stupid question is itself stupid. One might think, for example, of asking a man if he still beats his wife: if he answers "yes," he is guilty; and if he answers "no," he is also guilty.)

Jesus said, "From the days of our youth, we have been taught that we can know truth if we ask the right questions. One problem with this is that *people are in the habit of not hearing what they don't want to hear*, for they believe not what is true but what makes them happy.[30] Another problem with such thinking is that it is backwards—for questions are genuine when they are the effect, not the cause, of truth. I am here reminded of a parable from one of my distant relations."

"Supposing," said my relation, "that one must ask questions before knowing the truth is akin to a man who has been shot by a poisoned arrow. When attended to, the man said, 'I will not allow you to remove this arrow until I know of the one who shot me: whether he is fat or thin, rich or poor; I must know his name and clan, his ethnicity and his skin color, where he is from, what kind of bow shot the arrow, what kind of bird the feathers came from, and the kind of wood that the shaft was made from.'"

Jesus then said, "Dying people, who don't have time for silly questions, would shout, 'Get the arrow out!' Even if one might say with Job, 'The arrows of the Almighty are in me, my spirit drinks in their poison,' such a one would cry to God."

As if they did not hear him, the friends of the Samaritan woman then asked another question (they were like a leaf which endlessly swirls in an eddy). "Is it not true," they asked, "that salvation comes from the Samaritans?"

Jesus answered, "Supposing that one religion holds the truth of God is akin to a Jewish man who has a poisonous arrow lodged in his breast but says, 'I do not want the arrow to be removed by a Samaritan; I only want a Jewish priest to do so. Yes, *truth is an arrow and the gate is narrow that it passes through*; but people who know that they are dying don't have infantile understandings of truth.[31] Religions are, at best, pointers to Truth; and *the only doctrine that Truth knows is faith expressing itself in love.*[32] The Son of Man lives and dies for others, and insofar as people assimilate his teachings, they live in Truth."

Vignette 14

Theresa and Simple Matthew

LITTLE THERESA, WHO LIVED in a hamlet just east of Eden, was playing in the street when she overheard women saying that Jesus would be preaching from a boat the next evening. When Theresa finished playing, she hurried home and asked her parents if she could go to see the spectacle. Theresa's skinny father thought that this was a good idea. Her mother also consented, but only on the condition that her elder brother would accompany her. The brother agreed—but he, too, had a condition: Theresa was to do his chores in the morning. As she promised, she awoke and did her brother's chores, and then her own as well. She went to the seaside early to ensure that she would have a good space. (It did not take much to prompt her brother, for going early enabled him to be free from doing other chores.)

Jesus arrived in the early evening. Because he was not in a rush, Jesus started to mingle with the crowd—even getting in a water fight with some of the children. Various onlookers expressed their dismay at such unbecoming behavior: "Holy men," a statuesque woman said, "do not act in this way."

Jesus then invited Theresa and her brother to join him in the boat. Both children happily consented; and Theresa took the bow while her brother sat in the stern. After the children had paddled out and weighed anchor, Jesus began to preach.

Theresa was not interested in what Jesus had to say. She only wanted to witness the oddity of a man preaching from a boat; but Theresa did re-member two things that Jesus said that evening: people should be care-free "like flowers of the field"; and "unless one becomes like a little child, one cannot please God."

As she aged, Theresa's simple faith was challenged—not least by her husband, Abel.

As a new convert, Abel was devout, and especially so in his marriage. His concerns were with his wife's welfare. Abel seemed to have a holy self-ishness that said, "If you make others happy, you yourself will be happy," and so every day he would ask Theresa, "Are you happy?"

Abel's happiness was furthered with the birth of his son, Matthew. For several years Abel had been an exceptional father—which was not always easy, for Matthew was mentally challenged. Abel hoped to instill in Matthew the truth of Judaism. Initially, this was beautiful and simple—for even as he taught Matthew stories, visited the synagogue, and celebrated the festivals, he modeled virtues; but a shadow lurked behind such blessedness, for as time wore on Abel became interested in *matters of great consequence*—especially how to defend the faith.[33]

Unbeknownst to himself, part of Abel's motivation for defending the faith was to help him feel better about himself. Even as a child, Abel had had a poor self-image. Schoolchildren picked on him because he was mentally slow and uncoordinated, and they tirelessly reminded him that his name means "mist" or "nothingness" (he felt like Aeneas who had been hidden from others in a mist). When Abel became an adult, others similarly regarded him as an underachiever. He never seemed to have his own story, and his life was interpreted through the lives of others. ("*Is there anybody going to listen to my story?*" he would ask.)[34] As a consequence, Abel desperately wanted to show others that he needed to be taken seriously, and that *his thoughts were too expensive to keep.*[35] One might have thought that Abel would have found himself when he married Theresa, for she was encouraging and supportive; but just the opposite happened, for the high regard that Abel had for Theresa accentuated the disregard that he had for himself. Abel wished that he was *so very special* like her, but he *couldn't look her in the eye*, for he regarded himself as a corpse without a name.[36]

This self-disregard seemed to dissipate when Abel met a man who challenged him to make his belief rational. This man told Abel that "*while physical training is of some value, mental training has value for all things—holding promise both for prestige and honor.*"[37] Quoting Socrates, the man said that "the unexamined life is not worth living."

From the little that Matthew could gather, it seemed that big words, ideas, and names of different people must be very important—for his dad could not stop talking about them. Matthew noticed that the more that his father became engrossed in names, terms, and concepts, the more his father became confused: his father *talked without meaning anything in particular (the way grown-ups often do)*.[38] Matthew was also confused. It seemed to him that the important thoughts caused friction between his mom and dad, and he didn't care about who was "right" and who was "wrong"—he just wanted to play.

Most every day, while Abel was occupied with matters of consequence, Matthew and Theresa would go for a walk. For Matthew, such outings were adventures that were charged with wonder. Matthew was *dazzled by the beauty of it all*.[39] On one walk, mother and son were slowly making their way up a hill. As they did so, Matthew stopped to stuff his tiny pockets with various treasures. His pockets were, in short order, burgeoning with oddly shaped leaves, twigs, and pebbles. Theresa smiled at this, yet she pulled his hand gently to coax him to go further up the hill. Matthew thought to himself, "there must be something very interesting at the top of the hill, for why else would mommy urgently want me to get there?" Matthew needed time to explore, to feel the breeze that swayed the grasses, to observe the insects crisscrossing the path, and *to listen to the growing of the trees*.[40] As for Theresa, she was lost in thought: she was perplexed about what her husband was missing, and she wondered what she could do. Theresa's train of thought was, thankfully, interrupted when Matthew bent over to inspect something growing beside a log. As before, Theresa gently tugged at his wrist. This time Matthew said, *"you don't have to worry because I'm not in a hurry at all."*[41]

During another walk, Matthew stooped down to pick up a feather. In his excitement, he showed the treasure to his mother. When the two of them sat down to drink some water, they looked at the feather more closely. While Matthew was happy just to wave and flex the feather, at the behest of his mother, he noticed that the feather was shiny on one side and dull on the other. The shiny side had many shades of brown and black in stripes and in flecks, and it glistened in the sunlight. Theresa explained to Matthew that this feather was from a male bird, which used its beauty to attract the less beautiful female birds. She went on to say that this is an oddity, for it is typically the female that is more attractive than the male. Theresa stopped her analysis when she noticed that Matthew had little interest in it: he wanted to use the feather as a fan.

Because Theresa was a novice in the spiritual life, she thought that she needed to explain everything, "for," she thought, "one's wonder will be enhanced if one has a knowledge of creation"—but the Reverend Doctor Matthew knew better.

Matthew then picked up a nut close to where he had found the feather. He wanted to see what was in the nut, so Theresa cracked it open. Much to the shock of Theresa and the delight of Matthew, there was a worm inside. Matthew asked how the worm got into the hard nut. Theresa started to explain that while the nut was soft and tiny a moth layed eggs on it. Before she could finish her explanation, Matthew, who had *so many other curious things to think about*, gave his attention to a squirrel that was cautiously making its way toward them.[42]

Because of the noise of Theresa's ongoing explanation, the squirrel scurried up a tree. The Reverend wiped his nose on his sleeve and then said, "Mommy, *you talk too much*"—even as he thought, "*the chief fault of grown-ups is that they always think of uninteresting explanations.*"[43] (Far from being humiliated by this innocent chastisement, Theresa felt blessed to be reminded of what is important.)

The kind of analysis that Matthew liked concerned his sensations and feelings. Matthew said, "*Mommy, I wanna feel sunlight on my face.*"[44] He then expanded this statement: "*As I open up my heart, the sunshine on my shoulders makes me happy and on the water it looks so lovely.*"[45]

As iron sharpens iron, Theresa and Matthew helped each other. Once, when Matthew started to attend school, the two of them walked through a field. Matthew asked his mother why he is different from others. Theresa wisely said that he was a beautiful little flower. He may not ever be a large flower that is in bloom for a long time, but that is okay, she said, "*for God loves little flowers that may never be seen as much as big flowers that stay in bloom.*"[46] In the weeks that followed, Matthew pondered over the flower teaching—such that the topic naturally came up while they were walking in the forest one day. Matthew again asked his mother why he was different. (This question was loaded for Theresa, for it reminded her of her own question. "Why," she would ask herself, "do I fret about things that are beyond my control?") Prior to answering his question, Theresa asked Matthew to guess how many leaves were on the forest floor. She then invited him to hold one such leaf. As he did so, Theresa pointed out its different veins that fed many smaller veins, the curvature of its edges, its striations, and its decay—especially where it was moist. "Every leaf on the forest floor," Theresa said, "is different. God uses many different ingredients to create beauty." Theresa then continued, "*every blade of grass, every insect, ant and golden bee,* even though they may not know it, *bear witness to the glory of God.*"[47] "Even so, your difference equally testifies to the glory of God. Everybody must do his part—be they *philosophers or plowmen*[48]—and *your part*[49] is to be lovely you."

Matthew then raised his eyes from the forest floor to the puffy clouds. Theresa asked him what he saw, and with great confidence he pointed and said, "there is Leviathan playing with another sea monster: *great big love is sweeping across the sky.*"[50] Theresa seized on this opportunity to talk about how small humanity is: "while the clouds are big to us, they are only tiny mists in a vast cosmos." Like his mother, Matthew then became philosophical: "Mommy, what is beyond the sky?" Theresa answered, "beyond the sky is a great canopy that is holding back the waters." Matthew then asked, "but what is beyond the great canopy?" Mommy said, "*that is where God lives.*"[51] Matthew then left his philosophical deliberations to remove a twig from his sandal.

Matthew was then tired and so he lied down in the grass. Theresa did not want to move from brilliant metaphors concerning tininess, so she invited Matthew to peer into the patch of ground. The two of them inspected the decaying foliage, the new sprig, and *the tiny ant that was making its difficult way through the undergrowth.*[52] For Matthew, it was as if all *eternity could be seen in a grain of sand, and a heaven in a wild flower.*[53] While Theresa was happy that Matthew could see eternity in the patch, what she really wanted him to see is that *humanity is between two infinities*—the heavens above and the ground beneath.[54]

It would be an oversight to think that Matthew's sense of wonder only applied to nature, for he was also intrigued by what he witnessed in the market: the aromas, the flies that swarmed on the meat, and people *with their hands full of little packages and their minds full of little packages*—like diminutive sparrows that mindlessly flit from branch to branch.[55]

One person who caught Matthew's attention was a heavy woman. Before Theresa could stop him, Matthew approached the woman and said, "You are the fattest person that I have ever seen." Various onlookers snickered, the woman herself grinned embarrassingly, and Theresa pretended not to hear at all.

While Matthew and Theresa rested in the market to enjoy a treat, Theresa marveled: "*No guru, no method, no teacher; just you and I and nature and the Father.*"[56] Theresa then thanked him, saying, "*you opened my eyes to the beauty I see.*"[57] Matthew had learned that when someone says "thank you," he was to respond with "you are welcome." He therefore mechanically said, "you are welcome." (His mother's thankfulness puzzled him, for it did not occur to him that others could not see beauty the way he could—*to the pure, all things are pure.*)[58] "Adults are strange," Mathew thought to himself, "for they love to make all kinds of silly distinctions: smart and stupid, fat and thin, *us and them.*"[59]

After nibbling on his treat, Matthew asked Theresa what "matters of great consequence" were. Theresa knew that behind this question was Matthew's puzzlement over his father, so she prayed as she spoke. Theresa said, "'matters of great consequence' are things that adults think are very important, but children know are not." Theresa said, "Your father *doesn't know what he is missing.*[60] He thinks that he will only be happy when he first attends to matters of great consequence. You and I know better, but he must learn that what is important is what is before him, not the many questions that he thinks are important." Matthew said, "Dad, then, is like a little flower that wants to be a big flower." "Yes, honey, that is exactly right," Theresa said. "Dad doesn't know it, but *he is both beautiful and empty*—beautiful because he is a creation, but empty because he is trying to be something that he is not.[61] The important thing is not to be a big flower, but, as flowers naturally do, *to catch the smile of God out of the sky.*"[62]

As only a loving mother can do, Theresa then noticed that Matthew was overtired. She thought that she had best get him home for a nap, lest he have a tantrum (which might be more embarrassing than calling the woman fat). As they were returning home, Matthew told his mother that Persephone had done a great job in painting the flowers. Theresa was not tempted to correct his theological inexactitude. "If," she said to herself, "Matthew lives in beauty, he is living in truth."

(Theresa had often noted to herself that Abel was lost not because he was not theologically exact, but precisely because in the very attempt to be theologically exact he had forsaken Truth: he wanted a system, but he sacrificed Truth to get it. Indeed, if he had been more reflective, Abel would not have turned to Theophilus to learn about the Socratic aphorism. He would have turned to his son, who daily proved that Socrates was wrong:

while Matthew was unable "to examine life" in any intellectual manner, in his simplicity he experienced beauty every day.)

Sometimes adults query over what is best. "Is it best," they ask, "to know the truth and be unhappy, or to be happy in a lie?" Matthew's life overturned such a mindless dichotomy, for he was altogether happy in the Truth—even as adults are unhappy in lies.

All the same, just as a river changes as it is fed by streams, and like the faith of his mother, Matthew's simple faith was challenged. In his teenage years, Matthew said to himself, "*When I was young, it seemed that life was so wonderful, a miracle, oh it was beautiful, magical; and all the birds in the trees, well they'd be singing so happily, oh joyfully, playfully watching me.*"[63] As Matthew grew older, however, society tried to teach him a better way: "*they showed me a world where I could be so dependable, oh clinical, oh intellectual, cynical.*"[64] While Matthew was never duped by the shallowness of society, his thinking nevertheless evolved. At first he thought that all things were themselves enchanted; he later thought that creation was imbued with the divine—such that *God came to him in the rustling grass of a summer breeze.*[65] As he grew older and more sophisticated, Matthew nevertheless grew in his awareness of the thin space between the heavens and the earth: he saw *the presence of God* equally in everything and in all circumstances—however mundane or sublime they might be.[66]

Vignette 15

Theophilus and Nobody

A RICH MAN FROM Carthage named Theophilus believed that pleasure was the highest good. The pleasure that he sought, though, was not that of Epicurean philosophy, for Theophilus was an unreflective hedonist—someone who, like a zombie, is dead even while he lives.

The life of Theophilus was tragic for his mother, Eunice. Eunice had named her son Theophilus because she was hoping that he would be a friend of God; but Theophilus had no interest in the gods, for he prided himself in the Epicurean view that deities, if they exist, were unconcerned with the affairs of humanity. (The truth of the matter, though, is that he did not believe because doing so would not add to his pleasure.)

In the evenings, Theophilus went to the gymnasium and then to the baths.

While at the gymnasium, Theophilus liked to lift weights where he was most visible to others; but, because of nearsightedness, he could only see himself—other people were blurred.

(Coupled to his myopia was the discomfort that Theophilus had with light; but his was not an insurmountable problem, for he structured his daily routine around darkness and light. He slept during most of the day; in the evenings he went to the gymnasium and the baths; and in the late hours of the night he did his reading, writing, and thinking.)

Darkness had already enveloped the streets when Theophilus made his way from the gymnasium to the baths (the only lights were from the heavens and from under a synagogue door). As he strutted along, his every step had a spring to it (not unlike cantering steeds at the games). Such self-confidence compelled him to focus on his shadow from the moon's light. The shadow was unlike any other, he thought, for it accentuated his brawny physique. He nevertheless wanted to overtake the shadow. Doing so was altogether reasonable, for everything else submitted to him. Why not his shadow? He was exceptional, beyond the pale of boring humanity: he was richer, stronger, more intelligent—in a word, unique; but the shadow refused to submit. When he turned down another street, he similarly found that he was *being followed by a moonshadow*; this gladdened him, "for," he said to himself, "while I am not able to overtake the shadow, the shadow nevertheless follows my lead."[67] After his return trip from the baths, the moon was higher in the sky—such that his form did not cast a shadow. "This is okay," he thought, "for Plutarch rightly said that the dead cast no shadows."

While at the baths, Theophilus discussed this or that esoteric point of the philosophers. "*Aristotle, Socrates, Plato,*" he said . . . "*morons!*"[68] Theophilus was particularly fond of chatting about Plato's cave analogy. According to Plato, people are chained to a wall in a cave. A fire that casts shadows on the wall is behind the people. The shadows are of reality, but because people can only see the shadows, they think that the shadows themselves are reality. Seeing reality for what it is requires becoming free of the chains, and to be free one needs to know that everything in this world is illusory. (Theophilus here would quote Lucretius: "life is a struggle in the dark.") Theophilus was similarly enamored with mathematical thought—that of Euclides, Parmenides, and other mathematicians. He also wrestled with the paradoxes of Zeno that suggest that motion does not exist.

At the baths there was a special room that euphemistically had the word "massage" over its doorframe. Theophilus pranced into the massage parlor like a lusty stallion. Some of the mares then *dreamed* that he would choose them—but nevertheless tittered among themselves when he gazed at himself in the *mirror*, saying that *he was vainly giving substance to shadows as he had done before*.[69] After Theophilus betrayed his conscience, he greeted the lord of the parlor with a kiss and paid his debt of 30 silver pieces. He then fell headlong in passion with one of the female servants. He referred to her as "that one" (her only deformity was a slight limp). After that one massaged him, she lathered his god-like physique with oil. She then removed her tunic, and the two of them spent the next moments dallying in the promptings of Venus.

Theophilus then returned home, where he spent hours in research. One subject that he often visited concerned the paradoxes of Zeno. Zeno had noted that if Achilles gave a tortoise a head-start in a foot race, even though Achilles is much faster than the tortoise, Achilles would never catch the tortoise. The reason is simple: Achilles would first have to run half the distance between himself and the tortoise, and to do so he would have to run half that distance, and to do so he would have to run half that distance, and on and on: Achilles would not only not catch the tortoise, he wouldn't even leave his starting position! Theophilus was disturbed over this paradox. "On the one hand," he reasoned to himself, "the conclusion of Zeno is inescapable; but on the other hand, experience tells me that I can go from A to B, that motion exists."

Theophilus researched what others had to say about Zeno's paradox, but he was unsatisfied with their answers. On one night, however, during the hour just before dawn, Theophilus had a moment of brilliant clarity. He then scribbled his definitive answer down and went to bed contentedly. But when he awoke that afternoon, he became frantic because *he could not find the papyrus on which he had scribbled the definitive answer.*[70] Theophilus forgot about finding the papyrus when another idea came to him. "If," he thought, "motion does not exist, it would be impossible for me to think, for thinking involves motion from one idea to another idea." "But," he dejectedly acknowledged, "this only shows that motion exists in the mental world; it has nothing to say about motion in the real world." Theophilus then said to himself, "Perhaps the answer to the paradox is that truth is not always reasonable. Maybe the unthinkable is what is most thoughtful: perhaps reason itself is *weak and untrue.*"[71] Theophilus was flustered. While the undermining of reason was itself reasonable, Theophilus did not want to remove this unknown god from its lofty throne—for reason had given him much pleasure.

The frivolous manner in which Theophilus studied philosophy was similarly expressed in his relationships. Theophilus viewed others as means through which he could achieve greater pleasure (not "through whom" because he thought of people as objects).

While at the baths one day, a man with an impressive looking mustache suggested that there is more to love than self-gratification. Theophilus was mystified. Because he had heard this kind of sentiment before, and in order to explore the idea further, Theophilus wanted to experiment. Theophilus said to a loose woman from Magdala, "*Wild thing, I think I love you; I wanna say that I love you, but the words don't seem to fit in my mouth.*[72] Live with me for two weeks so that we can learn about love." In spite of her initial lack of confidence, the woman agreed to the experiment.

After a few days into the experiment, Theophilus was puzzled about the woman, for he glimpsed in her something that he had never seen before. There seemed to be in her a beauty that went beyond her body, a beauty that was not even known to her, a beauty that wanted to develop, a beauty that attracted him. This beauty startled him—for the first time he felt drawn to a woman for something other than his urges. Such feelings frightened Theophilus, and he didn't know what to do with them. Theophilus then queried, "*Is this love that I'm feeling?*"[73] While in this confused state, *in which he mistook lust for love*, the whisper of beauty was nevertheless seen in the ways that Theophilus referred to the woman (he did not feel comfortable using her name).[74] While at first, Theophilus referred to her as "wild thing," as he became infatuated he referred to her as "baby" and other endearing titles. He said to her, "*Oh baby you're the only thing in this whole world that's pure and good, and wherever you are there's always gonna be some light.*"[75] Theophilus had glimpsed beauty, but he did not know how such beauty could be furthered. It was out of such confusion, that Theophilus trepidly confessed to this baby, "*when I was young I never needed anyone, and making love was just for fun, but those days are gone.*"[76] He therefore followed the only thing that he had confidence in: those instincts that had chained him to the wall.

Supposing that he had done everything well, and with only one night remaining in the experiment, Theophilus asked the woman, "Did I love?" Because the woman did not herself know what love is, she said, "We had amazing sex together, but we did not make love." Theophilus asked, "What, then, is love?" The woman dejectedly responded: "I don't know what love is; but I know what it is not: *all that I know about love is how to live without it.*"[77]

The woman became agitated because she seemed to know more about love than Theophilus did: "*You have sight, but you don't have any vision.*[78] The darkness within you has cast a spell over your mind, and I *don't wanna see your shadow no more.*"[79] Partly in order to justify herself, the woman from Magdala continued with tangled insults: "Worse than fornicating with your body is your philosophical fornication, for you lust after the acquisition of knowledge irrespective of goodness. You are not faithful to one grand idea, for you ogle every idea that passes before you; and when you equate truth with self-satisfaction, you intellectually masturbate. You are chained to one organ at the expense of another."

As if he didn't hear the flood of insults, Theophilus then said, "*we gotta make the most of our one night together before the final crack of dawn.*"[80] The woman complied, and the two of them frolicked together one last time. This time, though, to escape from the insufferable heat, they had to move to the root cellar—which was as dank and stench-filled as Tartarus. (The frolicking itself amounted to meaningless repetition rather than harmony—as mindless and blind as a donkey that turns stones.)

The experiment proved to be a disastrous failure when the woman farted during his orgasm. The woman laughed hysterically at this. "Is nothing sacred?" Theophilus thoughtlessly ejaculated. "Cursed woman!" he shouted. "It's as if seven thundering demons came out of you!" Theophilus was nevertheless thankful that the flatulence was not accompanied by odor (any odor quickly intermingled with the smell of other rancid slabs of meat in the cellar that had similarly not served their purpose in giving pleasure).

The parting shot of the woman was more cutting than her fart: "Both of us have a *malady of death*, for we are enslaved to ourselves; we want to love and be loved, but neither of us knows how this might happen."[81] Theophilus was *dazed and confused* by what the woman from Magdala said, for the light of her words again pierced his dark mind—yet, to make himself feel better, he concluded that *her soul had been created below.*[82] "*No where lives a woman true and fair,*" he proudly said to himself.[83]

One of Theophilus's acquaintances from the gymnasium was a socially awkward man named Abel. While at the beginning each man just needed a work-out partner, as time wore on physical concerns gave way to mental matters.

Years earlier, Abel had witnessed the martyrdom of devout Jews. This experience had a profound affect on him. The peace of the dying martyrs attracted him. Abel wanted that shalom, and so he committed himself to Judaism: he recited the shema and various psalms every day, and he had himself circumcised.

But the faith of Abel lost its lustre when he sought to convert others to the Hebrew faith. This was a difficult task for most everyone in his society was Roman (and therefore shaped by Greek thought), and Hebrew thought was very different than Greek thought. Abel consequently sought to defend his faith by trying to blend the two ways of thinking. While Abel had the best of intentions, he failed in this task even before he began, for the Greek thought of which Abel was acquainted was principally concerned with mental reality—it had little place for real existence.

Another way that Abel sought to defend his faith concerned the scriptures. Much of the scriptures were enriching, but other parts were problematic, even embarrassing: the divine sanctioning of genocide; the all-too-human presentation of God; and various other verses—like the one, for example, about God smearing dung on faces. Abel worked around such problems through ingenious interpretive methods. His most common assertion was that underlying the obvious meaning of any text was a spiritual truth—the violence that one reads about, for example, is ultimately about violence against individual sin. Another interpretive strategy that Abel used included his use of big words. He was particularly fond of the word "anthropomorphism." Abel loved this word because it was so long. "Yes," he confidently said, "the scriptures teach that God breathes, forgets things, is surprised, and is jealous because they were written 'anthropomorphic-ally'—so that humans can understand God." The fact that few knew what this word meant also lent credibility to Abel's assertions. While some of *his adversaries were frightened into conviction by how he thundered out rattling terms,*[84] others said, "*big words don't do no good, for they don't take the place of thinkin'.*"[85]

While the relationship that Abel had with Theophilus was initially functional, it became more mental as the two of them bantered about various thoughts. Because they were both hulking figures, and because they often argued about Greek versus Hebrew thinking, members of the gymnasium referred to them as "Hercules and Samson." (Theophilus liked this comparison, for it suggested that the members were impressed by his physique. In private, however, many such members mockingly said that Theophilus was more like the blinded giant who ate others in a cave— "Polyphemus" by name—while Abel was like the challenger of Polyphemus, a man called "Nobody.")

After months of debate, Theophilus destroyed all the arguments of Abel in three words: "truth is simple." "If," Theophilus contended, "you need to conduct all sorts of maneuvers in order to substantiate your belief system, your belief system must not be true." What Theophilus had said was devastating. Abel started to think that the whole edifice that he constructed was like a house built on sand, and he eventually renounced his faith. But this is not altogether true, for Abel did not turn from his faith when he realized that he could not rationally defend it. Abel became faithless much earlier, when he turned from life-giving trust to forcing faith into a system. It was in his strenuous effort *to justify the ways of God to men*[86] (that is, *to help God across the road like a little old lady*)[87] that he had abandoned God.

Abel was nevertheless religious in his irreligion, for various heart-felt convictions remained intact. One way in which the faith that Abel had renounced still clung to him is with respect to his attitude toward Theophilus. Abel surmised that Theophilus had a negative philosophy: "I must be right," Theophilus suggested, "because others are so wrong." Consistent with this, Theophilus did not provide Abel with a life-giving alternative. Abel, who desperately wanted a positive answer, said to himself, "*When I left I didn't know what I was leaving behind, or what I was hoping to find.*"[88] Abel then felt guilty for the resentment that he had for Theophilus. The way that he atoned for such guilt was, sadly enough, by spending more time with Theophilus. Another way in which the faith that Abel had renounced still clung to him concerned social conventions: the innocent question, "how are you?" reminded Abel that *he was responsible for all people*, that he was "his brother's keeper"—an ethical imperative that he could not renounce so easily as his religion.[89]

As is often the case with people who turn from religion, Abel became jaded. Whereas he had used the psalms to enrich his faith, he now recited them to express his cynicism: twisting the Shepherd Psalm, he could say, "*I curse your rod and staff; they no longer comfort me.*"[90] Such cynicism came out rather crudely in his jesting with Theophilus. On one occasion, Theophilus said that "to know oneself" is the goal of philosophy. Abel seized upon this moment to explain that the Hebrew verb "to know" often means "to have sex with." Abel facetiously concluded that, far from being the goal of philosophy, "to know oneself" is to have sex with oneself. At another time, while they were at the gymnasium together, Abel gibed Theophilus. Quoting the prophet Ezekiel, Abel said, "Your penis is like that of a donkey." Complementing this scripture with a Roman story, Abel went on, "Your penis is like the penis of the man that became enormous when the man became a donkey." Not to be undone, Theophilus retorted by saying that Abel's member had been mutilated—even likening Abel's circumcision to the violent castration of Uranus. Abel laughed at this rejoinder, but he did so nervously—for he was ashamed of his circumcision. While initially the circumcision separated him from unbelieving humanity, it had since become embarrassing—he even asked a surgeon if flesh could be sewn onto his penis in place of his lost foreskin. (More poignantly, the rejoinder of Theophilus reminded Abel about his lost faith—which was much more painful than losing his foreskin.)

Theophilus had experienced much pleasure, and then life happened. While repairing a leak at his mother's house, Theophilus lost his balance and fell off a stool. He thought nothing of it at the time; but over the weeks that followed, he noticed that his limbs were losing strength. Eunice, his mother, urged Theophilus to see a renowned physician—*Iban ben Ilyich* by name.[91] Iban's diagnosis was dire: Iban babbled about how the loss of strength may well spread to other parts of his body; but his three-word analysis said it all—"you are dying." At such words, Theophilus looked like a blind man whose sight was suddenly restored but whose vision was overcome by brilliant light.

(Theophilus complained to Eunice about the physician's obtuseness; but he then noted that the way that he himself had diagnosed Abel's philosophy was how Iban had diagnosed his body: he had thought that Abel's problem was only mental, as something that could be fixed if only correct syntax was used. It did not occur to Theophilus that Abel was an individual who had feelings. As Theophilus reflected further on the matter, he concluded that he had also treated the woman from Magdala in a similar way—not as a person, but as an object, as a means to his own ends.)

At first, Theophilus denied that he was dying: "the cosmos needs me," he would say. When Theophilus could deny it no more, he became angry—such that he would get offended easily when someone slighted him or did not agree with him. The anger of Theophilus was colored by despair, for he had no one to which he could direct his anger. "It would," he thought, "be inconsistent to get angry at gods that don't exist."

Much to the chagrin of Theophilus, Iban's diagnosis proved to be coming true: he could no longer coordinate his limbs, and he lost strength in both hands. Theophilus no longer gazed with pride at his Herculean physique—even as he lamented, *"I'm not half the man I used to be; there's a shadow hanging over me."*[92] Furthering his despair was the fact that life went on as usual. Most everyone at the gymnasium had learned that Theophilus would no longer be coming because he was dying. Theophilus assumed that, with such news, time would stand still, that things would not be the same, that people would have to adjust their schedules; but his absence was scarcely recognized—*tomorrow was as yesterday*.[93] Like the flickering of a fading wick, different thoughts flashed through his mind: "*I wish that I had remembered sooner that I would die*[94] . . . *I thought I'd have something more to say*[95] . . . I will exit not *with a bang, but a whimper*."[96]

For the first time in his life, Theophilus recognized that he was not unique. No, the cosmos did not need him. No, he was not indispensable. Like all people, he ate, excreted, grew tired, and was subject to illness; and like all people, he would pass away like a vapor. "No," he said, "I am not an invincible *eagle that soars above the sea*.[97] Far from enjoying the sunshine, I have become like Icarus plummeting down to dark waters—only Icarus is remembered. Were I to write a story about myself, I might use the title *Chronicles of Wasted Time*,[98] for *I have fritted away the hours in an offhand way*.[99] I agree with what my cousins will say: 'we are not uncomfortable about not being, but about never having been.' Indeed, *I have not only been dull myself, but I have been the cause of dullness*, for I have even made Nobody dull."[100]

Much of what Theophilus had emphasized in his studies similarly became loathsome: reason is good, he thought, but it has little to say about actual living. "I have been like an architect *who draws up plans for a mansion, but chooses to live in the cellar*[101]—even as this mansion exists *in a nowhere land*,[102] a land of ideas and concepts that waffle about in unreality. I have *made all my nowhere plans with Nobody*;[103] *and like a soap-bubble, my thinking burst when it alighted on an actual circumstance*."[104]

As much as the pain allowed him to do so, Theophilus revisited the philosophers in his (now scattered) mind. He recalled that Socrates had said something like "true philosophers make dying their profession," that many philosophers aspired to live "the good life," and that the goal of philosophy is "to know oneself." "Yes," he said, "self-knowledge is the beginning of wisdom." He then had an unreasoning impulse *to pray to the God that he'd always denied*:[105] "Oh, unknown God," he whimpered, "*kindly tell me who I am*."[106]

When Theophilus was sick in bed, those who came to see him did so out of a sense of duty. Some such people awkwardly expressed something, but their expressions were *as meaningless as wind in dry grass*, for they avoided matters that interest dying people.[107] Eunice was an exception, for she instinctively knew what her son needed. Eunice knew a man who had known Jesus since Jesus was a child and who had memorized dozens of his teachings. She brought this man to sit beside her ailing son. While the man had trouble communicating because he had a stuttering problem, one story gripped Theophilus in particular. When various religious leaders chastised him for hanging out with so-called sinners, Jesus said, "it is not the healthy who need a doctor, but the sick." As he tossed and turned in pain, Theophilus was mystified about this saying. "At one level," Theophilus thought, "the sinners are the sick; but at another level, those who thought that the sinners were sick are themselves sick." Because Theophilus was not able to think matters through in a sustained way, he caught truth in snatches (which is really how anyone catches it). Theophilus was puzzled over the prayer in which Jesus thanked God "for hiding the truth from the wise but making it known to the simple." The topic of relationships was impressed upon him when he thought of Jesus' words, "Do to others what you would have them do to you." "Yes," Theophilus thought, knowing oneself is the goal of philosophy, but I only know myself as I live for others: I am *not an island, entire of myself,* for I need people.[108] The walls of my cave have echoed my life: insofar as I have been indifferent to others, truth had been indifferent to me."

The more that he drifted in and out of consciousness, the more he was haunted by his own stupidity. His last words, which were not directed to anyone in particular, were like a prayer: "*Don't let the sun go down on me.*"[109] *His life then fled with a moan, to the shades*—the self-centered of whom were tormented, while, as the poet has said, the virtuous "exercised their bodies in a grassy gymnasium."

Only a handful of people came to dress the body of Theophilus, lay it in a tomb, and say what a wonderful person he had been (like most eulogies, such words were not true). Among the people who gathered were Eunice, Iban, the woman from Magdala, and Abel. Eunice said that Theophilus was a good son (but she wished that he would have confessed, "In your light, I see light"). Iban said that Theophilus was courageous in life and death, and Abel said that he was a great thinker. As they kindly denied the truth, a rooster crowed in the distance. Only the woman from Magdala heard truth in her silent pain—even as she grieved over what might have been but never was.

Vignette 16

A Grieving Widow

JESUS HAS RUINED MY life. I hate him. Jesus says that underprivileged people are more likely to trust in God. He is wrong. Yes, Jesus is wrong. My husband was recently killed by a Zealot, making me a widow, and I don't trust God. (What has God ever done for me?)

Not including the two who died in infancy, I have had four children: like his father, the oldest boy was forced to fight for Rome; my daughter works in a massage parlor; one of my sons is a drunkard; and my other son has abandoned me to follow Jesus. If Jesus was concerned about widows, he would have said to this son, "Go home and look after your mother"; but this did not happen. A few days before the funeral of my husband, my son listened to Jesus. My son was compelled to follow that maniac, but he first wanted to attend to funeral needs. Rather than saying something consoling, Jesus told my son, "let the dead bury their dead; come and follow me." My son did not even attend his own father's funeral! The scar under my son's eye is nothing like how his irresponsibility has pierced my heart. I was more angry at the funeral than I was sad: I kept thinking that sense would come to my son, that he would show up, that he would comfort me as I wept. My sister held my hand through the service, but it should have been my son.

I am angry with my son, but I am mortified by that preacher. My friends have confirmed just how seriously Jesus takes himself. I am told that he says that one must hate one's own life, and that one must gouge out one's eye or cut off one's limb if such body parts keep one from embracing his teachings. He similarly said, "I have not come to bring peace to the earth, but a sword that will divide family members from each other." What an egomaniac! Even Narcissus could learn from him! (Forgive me, Narcissus, if I have slighted you. While you equated your reflection with beauty, Jesus thinks that he reflects God—yet it is not the face of God that he sees, but his own love of self.)

I wonder what kind of relationship Jesus has with his own mother. I am sure that he will grieve her. Like Hades did to Demeter, and like my son has done to me, *he will pierce her heart with sorrow—as with a sword.*[110]

Vignette 17

Marcus and His Mother

I OFTEN FANTASIZED ABOUT killing my father. I told my mother that the world would be a better place without him, that he was a waste of skin.

While all of my siblings have also had problems with my father, my younger brother, who has since become a drunkard, had a particularly toxic relationship with him. I have been told that at my father's funeral my younger brother gave a bitter eulogy. In a most sarcastic manner, he inverted what is often said on such occasions. "My father taught me more than any other person how not to be," he said. While people at the funeral were scandalized by my brother's caustic words, they did not know my father. I understand my brother perfectly well.

On few occasions was my father physically violent; but what my father said was more hurtful than anything he ever did. I remember my little brother taking the donkey for a ride. The donkey slipped on the mud and gashed its knee, causing my brother to tumble into the ditch. My father then yelled at my brother, saying that he needed to pay the veterinarian's bill—but he never asked if my brother himself was hurt. Perhaps one of the most hurtful things that my father ever said is when he coldly told my mother about his relationship with a prostitute. At the time, I did not understand why my mother cried every day; it was only later that I understood. I hate him for what he said to her.

My mother is angry with me because I did not go to the funeral; but if truth be told, the fact is that she is most angry not with my absence but with the absence of my father throughout their marriage. (It is easy to blame the living.)

My mother may think that I ought to have comforted her at the funeral; but she herself gave me little comfort in life. What I mean is that she never taught me what the purpose of life is. She did not even show me what is most important in life. One conversation that I had with my mother comes to mind. I remember asking her, "*Which is the way I ought to go?*"[111] She cunningly answered, "*That depends a good deal on where you want to get to.*"[112] My mother knew what I was driving at. She knew that *I wanted someone to tell me clearly which way I ought to go*, why I was alive and how I should live; but because she herself did not know, she cloaked her answer in wisdom.[113] Even if my mother did have ideas, it would have been impossible for her to tell me, for she herself had been hurt by my father: because my father's life was meaningless and because my mother had been crippled by him, her life, too, amounted to nothing. My mother gave me life, but she herself did not have life.

Like my mother, my father never had life. One day he asked me what I wanted to do. I told him that I wanted to become an actor. He told me that I was deluding myself—"a pipe-dream, devoid of meaning," he said. This last point infuriated me most of all. Because of his hypocrisy, I stormed out of the house. What he said was akin to confused Solomon (who thought that everything is a chasing after the wind), rebuking Sisyphus for the meaninglessness of pushing a boulder up a hill only to have it roll down again. What a hypocrite! *All that my father left behind* is emptiness.[114] Now that my father is in Hades, he would agree with me about his hypocrisy (there may well be confusion in Hades, but there is no unbelief—everyone in Hades believes).

My absence from the funeral was consistent with my father's purposelessness, for I am now following someone who gives me purpose. On the night that I first met him, Jesus noticed that I was depressed. I then said to him, "*Jesus, Jesus, help me. I'm alone in this world, and a fucked up world it is too.*"[115] I then implored him, "*Jesus, Jesus, what's it all about?*"[116] He said that I will grow into the right answers as I occupy myself with life in the kingdom. While this answer mystified me, I am nevertheless confident that following Jesus will help me to understand life, even as doing so will enable me to forget the stupidity of my father. (I, too, may one day become a father, and while my father may have eaten sour grapes, my teeth will not be set on edge.)

Vignette 18

Martha and Naomi

PEOPLE IN THE COMMUNITY thought that Martha was a sophisticated and successful lady. Martha, who lived in a suburb called *Vanity Fair*, never had to worry about preparing a meal because she had a maid.[117] Martha also enjoyed the fact that she could do her own hair: she was most skilled at braiding and platting. She only told her maidservant to help when she was meeting someone distinguished. (The maidservant's hair was itself always tautly pulled back, lest it get in the way of work.)

While Martha was statuesque and beautiful, one thing that dismayed her was a small mole on her right cheek. Others referred to it as a beauty mark, but Martha thought that such people were only pretending to be nice. Martha did different things to hide the beauty mark, but none of her strategies was altogether successful. Applying oil did not work because doing so only made the mole glisten. While letting the bangs on her right side fall upon her cheek was an effective strategy, it could not always be used, for it limited the ways that she could style her hair—and she knew that others would eventually clue-in as to why she was doing this. Martha got into the habit of looking sideways so that her left cheek would be more visible than her right cheek. Like any habit, this one started simply; but it slowly became habitual for Martha to look sideways—such that her husband asked her if she had a sore neck, and Naomi (her twin sister) wondered if Martha's left eye had better vision than her right eye.

The way in which Martha fixated on what others thought may be particularly seen in how she protected the respect of her husband—a distinguished judge whose name was Daniel. While hosting guests, Daniel would twist his mustache—even as he was quick to tell them of his accomplishments. Martha disliked this (not his boasting, but how he played with his mustache, for she thought that *in matters of grave importance, style, not sincerity is the vital thing*).[118] Martha similarly liked the name Daniel (she liked it so much that she could not imagine being married to a man that did not have this name). This Hebraic name, which means "God is my judge," has an air of respectability about it, Martha thought, for while it is religious, it is neither impious nor showy like names that include the name of God—especially names that include "yah" (which is short for "Yahweh").

Martha was particularly fond of her twin sister. One difference between the two women was that Naomi was slightly more attractive than Martha: her facial features were more symmetrical, and she preferred to let her dark hair gently cascade upon her shoulders—rather than managing it in one way or another. Another difference is that whereas Martha had had no problem with bearing children, Naomi was barren. Martha and Naomi had a cousin named Marcus who followed Jesus. This did not surprise them, for since their childhood days Marcus had been concerned with motivations—such that he would say that one could do good things with bad intentions or bad things with good intentions. He told Naomi, for example, that while she ought not to have struck him under the eye when they were children, he harbored no bitterness against her—for she was but a child.

Marcus persuaded Jesus to stop in to see Martha. While Martha was honored that Jesus would be visiting her, she was perplexed because she did not think that she had enough time to make the proper arrangements: her maidservant would have to purchase food from the market (and she feared that this would give the maidservant one more thing to be angry about); and she needed to primp and adorn herself. Marcus and Jesus showed up as promised, and, contrary to the worrying of Martha, everything was ready—her maidservant had prepared an amazing spread, and Martha herself looked stunning. Marcus and Jesus then reclined, a servant washed their feet, and the maidservant gave them a refreshing drink (not just any drink, for it had bits of fruit floating in it). Niceties were then shared, followed by weather talk.

Martha seemed to be pleased with everything; but Naomi felt awkward, for she worried that both Marcus and Jesus would interpret things as being superficial. Out of her nervousness, Naomi told a joke: "While a congregation was emphasizing the importance of humility, the rabbi beat his breast and said, 'Woe is me, for I am undone; I am a sinner.' Not to be outdone, the president of the congregation then lay prostrate on the synagogue floor. He cried, 'I, too, am a sinner—for I have had impure thoughts.' When the custodian of the synagogue saw what the rabbi and the president said and did, he proclaimed that he, too, had been a sinner. At this, the president smugly said to the rabbi, 'Now look at who says he is a sinner.'" Both Jesus and Marcus laughed uproariously. Martha, who wanted to complement the mood, then laughed herself. The joke turned out to be serendipitous, for it naturally led the discussion to differences between inner beauty and outer beauty—a subject, Marcus thought, that Martha needed to hear.

Everyone was then invited to eat around a table. (Dining in this way was a definite sign of being avant-garde, for it was customary to serve food to people reclined on the floor.) Various "oohhs" and "aahhs" were then made: Martha commented about how the delicacies had been prepared and where they came from; and the maidservant had set the table exquisitely— everything was strictly assigned to its proper place. After they had eaten a little, Martha brusquely gestured to the maidservant to get more food (the maidservant could not do so quickly because she suffered from a bowed spine that caused one shoulder to droop). As she tightly clutched the dirty dishes, the maidservant obediently made her way to the kitchen.

Because he was uncomfortable with the silence, and hoping to force Martha to reflect on what he thought was her shallowness, Marcus started to talk about how whitewashed sepulchers could not hide death. Out of her ongoing nervousness, Naomi then interrupted him. "What," she asked Jesus, "do you mean when you say that 'people do not live by bread alone'?" Because Marcus was anxious to display his knowledge, he explained things: "by 'bread,' the master simply means 'the necessities of physical existence.'" The fact that Marcus interrupted made Martha a little angry; but rather than causing a scene, she only grimaced at him. Pretending that she had not heard Marcus's answer, Naomi then looked to Jesus. Jesus responded to Naomi's query: "People try to satisfy themselves by filling their physical appetites, but such appetites are never satisfied—for peace of heart does not come from things. When we pray, 'Give us this day our daily bread,' we recognize that we are reliant on the Father for everything—even as we know that others, like Martha's hardworking maidservant, are instruments of the Father."

Thinking that Jesus would readily concur with her, Martha then asked, "Rabbi, is it not true that one can only live for others if one first lives for oneself?" (Martha wanted others to see how very astute she was.) Jesus said,

"We only live for ourselves when we put others first. Insofar as we treat others the way that we want to be treated, we treat ourselves well." Jesus had noticed how Martha wanted everything to be just right, how she turned her face to hide the mole, and how she longed for acknowledgement. Jesus therefore continued: "When people live for the esteem of others they are unhappy—even ugly." (While both Naomi and Marcus nodded in agreement, neither of them understood that Jesus had used such words to help them as much as Martha.)

Vignette 19

Martha's Maidservant

"Martha is a bitch," the maidservant murmured through pursed lips. "Everyone in the community knows this—even if they pretend otherwise. Because I am with her every day, I know what kind of person Martha really is. When she has people over, she contributes to making food preparations, but only so that she can be praised. She also loves to be admired for her appearance. No doubt, she is a beautiful woman. She is statuesque, and complementing her loveliness is a beauty mark on her cheek—but her outward beauty is far more attractive than any beauty that might be within her. It seems to me, for example, that she is jealous of her sister, for she secretly delights in the fact that her sister is barren—a conclusion that I have drawn from remarks that she has made while I have done her hair."

"Yesterday a preacher from Nazareth came to visit with my (now estranged) nephew. At one point during the meal, Martha rudely gestured to me to replenish the food (as if I was a dog that needed to be shooed away). I was only too happy to comply—for I was glad to get away from such insufferable people. As I escaped to the kitchen, I continued to listen to the conversation. While much of it was muffled, I put the fragments that I heard together—and, to my horror, the preacher said that I was not responsible for providing daily bread."

"I hate Martha, but I also hate myself because I am artificial—for I have to pretend that I like her. When she says something that she thinks is important, I nod my head in agreement—even if what she is saying is complete nonsense. Making things worse is that I feel guilty for despising her. While Martha does things that could make a preacher swear, perhaps

I exaggerate how bad she is. Perhaps the hatred that I have of Martha is an outworking of the hatred that has grown in me (but even if I am hateful, it is not my fault—for I was born under an angry star)."

"Just before the funeral of my brother-in-law, my sister had the gall to scold me. She said that I am mean, and that I don't listen. This angered me. I wanted to say, '*before you accuse me, take a look at yourself*'—but because I knew that I needed to practice restraint at the funeral, I said nothing.[119] Yet I am right in thinking that my sister only said this because she herself is angry, and because she herself does not listen—all too often she projects her own shortcomings on others."

("'You do not listen,' she said. Oh the nerve of that woman! How little she knows! My listening is even accompanied by wisdom, for I know how to respond even before someone is finished speaking.")

"My sister recently likened me to a harried grade-school teacher who has shouted at naughty boys all day long—and is ready to explode. She said that I hated myself, that I was like a rooster fighting its own reflection, like a boxer striking his own shadow."

"I hate hate. Hate has no time to try to understand. Hate is impatient. Hate is rude. It boasts. It is proud. It seeks itself. It gets angry easily. It remembers the wrongs done to it. Hate makes all things disagreeable, even loathsome. Hate loves to have enemies: the Jews hate the Romans, who hate the Zealots, who hate the Pharisees, who hate the Essenes—and everyone loves to hate the Samaritans. Hate longs to control others. Hate loves to find faults in others—even as it rejoices in their downfall and is quick to overlook its own mistakes. Like a raging fire, hate consumes everyone that is before it."

"My sister told me that hate and perfectionism are linked, for the perfectionist hates what is imperfect. On this score, she is right. As stupid as she can be, sometimes she seems like a brilliant person—at which point, I always agree with her. After she spoke of perfectionism, for example, she told me of the related danger of expectations. Quoting a wise man, she said, 'deferred expectations make the heart sick.' When we want or even insist that people do things our way, and they inevitably fail, we become angry or frustrated. The answer, my sister said, is to rid oneself of expectations. I thought of her counsel when I had recently tried to show my daughter a better way to do the laundry. Between her hysterical sobbing, my daughter said, 'I try my best . . . , but everything I do . . . is not good enough for you.' My daughter then reminded me of the time that I was teaching her how to skip. She said that just as I had become quickly frustrated by her lack of coordination, so I was now being impatient about how she did the laundry. In the midst of her blubbering, she said that she could never meet my expectations. My son, who was there at the time, nodded in agreement. At the time, I chalked this up to teenage angst (their careless comments just seem to fall out of their mouths). I said to myself that they would one day think differently, that in the future they would be grateful for the expectations that I have of them. Maybe, however, my children are right; maybe I am too critical. Perhaps the anger that my sister accuses me of is related to my tendency to demand perfection. For a few weeks now, I have been working on trying to be less demanding. When my daughter was recently exasperated about her inability to do the laundry the way that I had told her, I told her to lighten up and take it easy. My daughter looked relieved when I said this, and my son smiled."

Vignette 20

Silenius, the Sober Scientist

LONG AGO, MY CHILDHOOD friend told me that one of his chums had molded twelve birds from clay, breathed into them, and then made them fly away by clapping his hands. My friend grew impatient with me when I did not believe him. "Clay is made of dead material," I said. "Life cannot come from clay." My thinking, however, has since changed.

I have always been intrigued by matter, and by how matter works with other matter. I was taught that things in the cosmos are an admixture of earth, air, fire, and water—"from the atoms of Democritus to the constellations of Anaxagoras," my teachers would confidently say. "It is the calling," they would say, "of natural philosophers to determine the degree to which these four elements intermingle in things."

Perhaps to the chagrin of my teachers, my thinking about unchanging elements has itself changed. Supposing that I know what a tree is because I know precisely how much of each element is within it, is, in my mind, painfully reductionistic, for having knowledge of parts of something is not at all the same as having knowledge of the whole of something. (This is akin to the action of Procrustes—reducing someone by cutting off their legs so that they might fit into what we think is best.) The thinking that something can be understood when we understand its parts is, similarly, not holistic, for we only know the parts of something as they function with other parts. In my mind, "four-element" thinking is similar to the actions of Herophilos who dissected humans to know humans: one dissects what is dismembered and dead, while one can only know life as it is lived. (Sorry Euclid, the idea that the sum total consists of adding up the parts only works in mathematics:

foolish minds, which worship the Gorgon of consistency, add up the parts but do not have the sum—even as they pontificate "It is!" and "It is not!")[120]

(Plato's world of ideas, in which individual things only exist as participants in absolute forms, is also not holistic. Take trees as an example. Plato said that individual trees exist insofar as they reflect the existing form of "treeness"—that presumably waffles about in no particular place with others "nesses" in the world of ideas. Contrary to such sophistry, individual trees are known when one witnesses how they interact with their particular environments.)

For the sake of clarity, I will repeat myself in a different way. Let's say that it is true that four elements underlie all things. Such truth would only be about the elements themselves. It has nothing whatever to say about how such elements interact with each other. The various ways in which fire might interact with water are infinite. This also holds for earth and air. Even if one had an encyclopedic knowledge of each element in things, such knowledge might (speaking very generously) only amount to 15 percent of all that can be known about matter. What, then, of the remaining 85 percent of the ways in which the elements interact with each other? We know very little, or even nothing, about this. More tellingly, it would be the height of hubris to assume that the 85 percent follows the same laws as the 15 percent. We can only appreciate the 15 percent that we do know as we stand back to see the whole scene. I think, again, of wood. If we think that we can rest after we have explained that wood consists of four elements, we must think again. Other questions that concern us are as multitudinous as the leaves on a forest floor. "How does this one tree interact with the shrub beside it?," "Why do only certain plants grow under this tree?," "How much water does this tree need every day?," etc.

On the same trajectory as such questions is the question of all questions, the telos question: "What is wood for?" Lest he lose sight of the forest for the trees, the interest of the natural philosopher must be governed by this question. It's as if matter points beyond itself and cries, "don't only look to me, but to what orders and sustains me—to what holds me and encompasses me." It's as if all reality was flowing toward something, and life's purpose is to become part of that current. No, matter is not all that matters: there is a world that exists in, through, and above the world of elements. It is this world that most captivates humanity—a world of goodness and beauty, which are no less existent than elements.

Unlike my friend Theophilus, I don't believe in Epicurean thought. In my mind, Democritus and Lucretius were on the right track when they insisted that one should study the natural world, but they lost their way when they concluded that pleasure is the chief end of humanity. So also, I don't believe in the message of the Cynics, who only make me laugh. It has rightly been said of them that they *gouge out the eyes of others in order to help them see better.*[121] Yes, they are correct that the traditions of society are often silly, but, having nothing positive to say, they devote their energy to debunking belief. Again, I don't believe in what the Stoics say. While they are correct that "humanity is born to suffer as surely as sparks fly upwards," not unlike the Cynics, they have little positive to say—for their emphasis is that wise people will resign themselves to injustice. Again, I don't believe in the cool and withdrawn thought of Aristotle (or his denizens of followers). It seems to me that his god is little more than a reflection of himself—a detached and unmoved mover.

"I don't believe," "I don't believe," "I don't believe." Is this my creed? I don't like it when people call me an atheist. I am a believing agnostic. It is not true that I don't believe in the gods. More properly, I don't believe in the gods as they have been depicted. What, with all their adulteries, connivings, and brutish displays of power, they are just like people. It is for the same reason that I don't believe in the Jewish God. While the Jewish stories tend to be more realistic than the Graeco-Roman myths, it seems to me that the dreadful violence in them is little more than the projection of humanity on God. At the beginning of the Jewish holy book, one reads Elohim saying that people are made in his image. This is a good start; but then all that is good becomes evil as people invert what Elohim said by making him in their own image.

What, then, do I believe? I believe that I should strive to be perfectly human. I believe that I don't need to believe to know, for imagination is more important than knowledge. I believe in wonder and beauty. I also believe that I must be intoxicated with life—a zest that is akin to drunkenness (it has been my experience that getting drunk on wine and being full of the Spirit are not unrelated, for both concern seizing life). For this reason, I don't like John the Baptist. John was on to something, but for whatever reason he ceased to be sparkling wine and became full of vinegar. He is altogether sober-minded about life, and he takes himself way too seriously—he could use a little fermenting! (There is, actually, little difference between the Cynics and John the Baptist: the one decries tradition, while the other decries living.)

The problems that I have with John are similarly present in his cousin, the so-called "messiah." While I was sharing a cask with my friend Theo in the market the other day, and as we were discussing various teachings of the philosophers, we overheard a young man say to John's cousin: "Jesus, Jesus, what's it all about?" The question was, in my mind, spot on, for most people exist without ever thinking about why they exist. To whom the question was directed, however, is another matter, for asking Jesus "what's it all about?" is like asking a blind man for directions. Jesus is anti-intellectual. How could he begin to know what life's all about? Jesus even said that God "has hidden truth from the wise and learned and revealed it to little children"—whatever that means.

Notwithstanding the problems that I have with both John and Jesus, it seems to me that, unlike most Graeco-Roman thought, they both think that history is going somewhere. Jesus often says such things as "the first will be last, those who exalt themselves will be humbled, mercy will be given to the merciful, judgment will be given to the judgmental, and God's will ought to be done on earth as it is in heaven." For Jesus, each "will be" implies an eventuality, an eternity that is to be participated in right now. (Perhaps this conviction is integral to the human condition, for the philosophers similarly teach that one participates in the Good as one is good.)

I asked earlier, "What is wood for?" Here is part of my answer: an individual tree does not exist for itself, but for the sake of every living thing in the forest. What holds for trees equally holds for life. "What is the individual for?" Individuals exist for the sake of others.

(Yes, I am a scientist, but I am also a pragmatist. When I ask, "what is the individual for?" I don't fixate on the elements of an individual, but on how individuals can help themselves by helping others. Can I prove that individuals exist for others? Certainly not. The slavish demand for proof may be likened to a fish not believing that it is in water until the existence of water can be proven. The fish is awash in water, even as all that exists is saturated in a *divine milieu*—a milieu that can only be known as it is lived in.)[122]

While my childhood friend was gullible in believing that his chum created birds from clay, I now think that he understood the world more than most natural philosophers.

Vignette 21

Zebedee, the Father of the Groom

ALTHOUGH JESUS HAD NOT been formally invited to the wedding, he happily accepted the verbal invitation of Zebedee, the groom's father. (Zebedee hoped that having Jesus at the wedding would rouse the ire of various guests.)

After the ceremony, many of the guests were singing and dancing while others were sitting on couches and sipping wine. Across from Jesus sat Zebedee. Trying to sound philosophical, Zebedee asked, "What is the basis of a happy marriage?" (Zebedee did not direct the question to any one person, yet he was hoping that Jesus would take the bait so that a scandal might ensue.)

Jumping at the opportunity to display his wisdom, a rabbi started off: "A key to any happy marriage is the submission of the wife. The story of Adam and Eve tells us as much, for it is only when Eve followed her own interests and did not 'listen to the voice of' her husband that they were cast out of the garden . . . " A studious looking young man then interrupted the rabbi. "I think that one should be careful when referencing the garden story, for we there read that Adam was 'with' Eve even while the serpent was deceiving her: Eve may have been deceived, but Adam said nothing when he ought to have dissuaded her." (The rabbi's wife, who had lived in abject submission to the rabbi, secretly delighted in how the young man challenged his argument.) Not to be undone, the rabbi continued. "You interrupted me. I did not say that submission is the only ingredient. I said that it is a key ingredient. There are other scriptures that teach the same thing." Not wanting to be bored by the rabbi's lifeless exposition of other scriptures, an unmarried girl said, "What about the man? Why is it always the woman's fault?"

At this moment many topics were on the table, yet with the hope that Jesus might say something controversial, Zebedee forcibly asked Jesus, "What do you think?" Before Jesus answered, he waited while those more interested in festivities than a theological discussion left—only to be replaced with new faces. Jesus then said the following: "Sorry, Zebedee, but I think that your question could be re-framed. Rather than asking, 'What is the basis of a happy marriage?' you might ask, 'What is the basis of a happy life?'"

Zebedee's hopes of creating a scandal were compromised when one of the guests then seized Jesus' arm and led him to the dance floor. One statuesque woman, who wanted others to think that she was as beautiful as she was pious, saw Jesus laughing and dancing with disreputable folks. While looking sideways, she said to the unmarried girl, "Jesus should not hang out with such folks; it is most unbecoming. *Who let all of this riff-raff into the room?*"[123] "Whatever do you mean by 'riff-raff'? These people are no different from anyone else, including you," the girl retorted. The woman was chaffed that the unmarried girl (who was not particularly beautiful), would dare to contradict her, so she moved on.

Meanwhile, additional wine had made Zebedee all the more desperate, such that he returned to the subject of a good marriage; but the more that people ignored him, the louder his voice got, and the more obnoxious he became. Zebedee then went on a disconnected rant about what he had heard others say. "Marriage is highly symbolic," Zebedee stammered before he belched, "for sexual union is akin to the union of the human soul and the divine Spirit." The people who listened laughed nervously. Upon being encouraged by the laughter, Zebedee had another gulp and quoted Socrates: "If you get a good wife, you will be happy; if you get a bad one, you will become a philosopher."

The statuesque woman then said, "You drunken fool. Holy people want to know what the sacred scriptures say about marriage." "Pardon me . . . you're right," Zebedee slurred, "we must understand marriage through the lens of holy scripture. Solomon, who was a righteous exemplar, had 300 wives and 700 concubines. He must have been very wise to keep all such women happy. (I only have one wife, and she is never happy!)" Prior to saying more, Zebedee guzzled what remained in his goblet. "While Solomon could have consummated each union, he could not have visited each member of his harem regularly. If he managed to meet different members of his harem three times per day, each one could have had sex only once per year. Did he even know their names? (But one cannot fault him for not knowing, for then he would be like the patriarch Jacob who, in his drunkenness, could not distinguish between buxom Rachel and flat-chested Leah). No, such women were sexually unsatisfied. It is no wonder that he himself wisely taught that 'it is better to live in a corner of a roof than with an ill-tempered woman.'"

Zebedee had managed to upset everyone at least once. He then stumbled away from the festivities, and contrary to his hopes to cause a scene, he only shamed himself.

Vignette 22

Levi, the Lover of Culture

WHILE I AM ILLITERATE, I do enjoy studying people. My wife doesn't like it when I watch others, for she gets jealous easily. For the sake of marital peace, I decided long ago that when I am with her it is best to keep my attention on her—but, sly man that I am, she is also an object of my investigations.

Even as I study my wife, I enjoy watching people haggle in the market. The purchaser might say, "This fruit is too expensive," and then she might wait for the seller to respond. The seller might then suggest a lower price or, if she is feeling confident, by defending the expensive price. The purchaser or the seller might then bluff—by walking away or by pretending to be in-sulted. The ordeal rarely has anything to do with what a fair price actually is, but much to do with besting the other.

The haggling that I see in the market is like all of life. It seems to me that from birth to death, people are acting out a play. The play is a tragedy. The only thing humorous about it is that the actors don't know that they are playing parts. Having a director is needless, because they say their lines perfectly. The actors are also most flexible, for each one plays many parts throughout the play. At first, the actor is the infant cooing like a dove and whose mother fawns over him with silly faces before she is forced to exit the stage when he pukes. When the actor again enters the stage, he is the naughty schoolboy, who does his utmost to win the favor of his father even as he ceaselessly teases other children. He exits that scene and re-enters the next as an idealist who berates compromise, only to become a lover who forsakes all sense and bows to his longings at the end of that scene. The actor finds himself on the stage yet again as an aged grandfather, *sans teeth, sans eyes, sans taste, sans everything.*[124] This is the last scene of all. In it, he finds that his eyes have grown dim (perhaps, he thinks, the lights from the orbs have darkened), his bones have become frail (such that the keepers of the house cause him to stoop), he cannot eat (because his grinders have become few), and he hears sounds that only exist in his atrophied brain. He has no interest in exiting this scene, for, quite unlike the scene in which he was a smitten lover, desire is no longer stirred; but he didn't need to exit anyway, for after *he had strutted and fretted his hour upon the stage,* he collapsed just before the curtain dropped.[125] The crowd who watched the whole play then stood to applaud the acting; but those who did not fall asleep, the reflective ones, did so nervously, for they knew that they themselves were the actors. Confirming this, the last words of the aged man were accusational: "you are the man."

How do we leave this play? *Must this show go on?*[126] We can only exit the play as we give ourselves over to another story, a story that was not written by empty society or lovers of self, but by the living God. It is only as we embrace this story that we become authentically ourselves and find ourselves joyously (but at times, awkwardly) at center stage. I said as much to one of my friends, but he said, "I will not attend the synagogue, because worshipers are hypocrites." He has often said that "*a believer is one who follows the teachings of God insofar as they are not inconsistent with a life of sin.*"[127] My answer to him has always been the same: "join the club; you would fit in perfectly . . . the human condition is itself hypocritical . . . if you can fog mirror, you are a hypocrite. " (I have been told that the word hypocrite was first used with reference to actors, for actors pretend to be someone else; but over time this word came to refer to religious people who pretend to be something that they are not.)

Another excellent place to study people is in the synagogue. Upon en-tering, one is confronted by a world that confronts the senses: "hallelujahs," prayer shawls, obeisances, incense, and holy furnishings. This world raises a host of questions for me, most of which concern the leaders of worship. Why do they wear garments that no other people wear? Why do they sit in Moses' seat while others sit on benches? Why do they use language that is seldom heard in daily discourse? While I myself attend the synagogue with conviction, I can't help thinking that the leaders of worship operate in their unreal world because they want power—the leaders receive their status not from who they really are, but from the props that surround them, especially their garments (*but a monkey in silk is a monkey no less*).[128]

(I am here reminded of what a rabbi friend told me. He said that he delivered an impassioned sermon; but no one listened to him—even suggesting that the speech was rather dull. Years later, he gave the same sermon to the same people, but this time everyone was enthralled. One difference was the clothes that he was wearing: he was commonly dressed when he gave the first sermon, but wearing clothes that suited his profession in the second sermon. My rabbi friend concluded that *it was not what he said that charmed his hearers, but the clothing that he wore.*)[129]

The people who come to worship are themselves little different from those who attend a theatre, for in both cases people are moved by the pageantry that they are beholding. The difference between the two is nevertheless stark: worshipers believe that what they are witnessing is a taste of the other-world; and when the show is over theatergoers resume their daily lives.

The danger with rites, vestments, and holy furnishings is obvious: people are easily deceived into thinking that they are as holy as the objects themselves. But this danger cannot be avoided, for not using such objects is also dangerous: because people are not disembodied spirits but are physical, it is important to adorn communal worship with holy objects—props that can be smelled, seen, touched, and heard.

This brings me to a discussion of prayer. Devout people often assume that if they use the correct words in the correct way, God will be compelled to act.

It is good to pray, "Almighty One, please give me deliverance from my distress." But better than this is to pray, "Almighty and Everlasting One, please grant deliverance from distress just as you granted the Hebrews in Egypt."

Why the second prayer is better than the first is that in addition to being "Almighty," God is also "Everlasting"; moreover, "grant" is less aggressive than "give"—even as the pronouns "me" and "my" are dropped (such pronouns may be suggestive of individualism). Finally, better than saying "give me deliverance from my distress" is saying "grant deliverance from distress just as you granted the Hebrews in Egypt"—for it would be inconsistent for God to deliver the Hebrews but not to deliver me. Honestly! Can God be manipulated by words and semantics? Infinitely better is simply, "Daddy, please give me a hand, for life sucks." It is not the words that are important to God, but the trust that infuses every word.

What I have said about holy objects and prayer may also be applied to the sacred text. It seems to me that synagogue leaders use the scriptures to control people: the better that they know the scriptures, the easier it is for them to maintain power.

One evening, hagglers in the market, theater-goers, and worshipers in the synagogue came together to listen to Jesus of Nazareth preach from a boat. I simply had to be there. I elbowed my way through the crowd until I came to a good vantage point. I then saw a little girl and her brother sitting in the boat with Jesus.

(I fondly recalled that this was the same little girl who had said to her skinny father, "look, daddy, *the rabbi is not wearing any clothes*."[130] Many people in the synagogue were shocked by such scandal; but I laughed. The girl knew that underneath the pretentious garb the rabbi was like everyone else: if she had been more cynical, she might have said, "*let's rip off his mask and see who he really is*.")[131]

I wondered if Jesus would hide behind a disguise; but I could not detect anything untoward in his manner. It seems that the words themselves were authoritative. Much of what Jesus said confused me, but I do remember him saying something like, "What you do to others is what you do to God." This is, I think, a goal of worship.

But I have to ask myself why I study others. What does this say about myself? When I look at others, it is like looking at my own face. It is only when I see myself in others that I can ever understand myself—and that I can ever hope to know God.

Vignette 23

A Christian Gnostic

MAKE NO MISTAKE, I love Jesus; but when I say "Jesus" I don't simply have in mind a Nazarene who slept when he was tired. When I say "Jesus" I think of the eternal Logos who governs the cosmos, and whose teachings mirror eternity—such that I pray, "O Jesus, you are Eternity." The teachings of Jesus are the keys that unlock the goodness of the universe: we only open the door to eternity when our lives reflect the Logos.

I am not always in agreement with so-called Christians who refer to me as a "gnostic"—as someone whose primary interest is experiential knowledge. As far as labels go, it is okay. (I would prefer, though, that the Christians don't refer to me as "gnostic" but as "a Jesus gnostic," for the special knowledge that interests me is knowledge that comes from embracing the teachings of Jesus.)

Many disagreements that I have had with so-called Christians concern how they use various words. This is not just a matter of semantics, for words are suggestive of what people think—even as Jesus said, "words are produced from the overflow of the heart." (My concern is a reflection of what I do for a living: I am a translator for Rome, which needs to know what conquered peoples say and think.)

Christians often equate, for example, the words "believing" and "thinking." Such an equation is a lexical confusion. Thinking has to do with reasoning out a conclusion on the basis of various facts. It is proper to say, for example, "I think that one plus one is two." When I make this equation, I start with an agreed upon definition of what "one" and "two" are. I then use reason to conclude that if I add one thing to another thing I have two things. I don't "believe" that this conclusion is valid: belief has nothing whatever to do with the equation.

(Did Jesus himself "believe" in God? This is an illegitimate question. It is like asking a boy if he believes that he must breathe when he runs; the boy would wonder why such a ridiculous question is asked. Jesus did not, properly speaking, "believe" in God; rather, he knew and experienced God.)

I am distraught by rumors that disciples of the apostles may draw up a creed. The proposed creed begins with "I believe." The creed reiterates this three times: "I believe in God. . .; I believe in Jesus Christ. . .; I believe in the Holy Spirit. . ."

(If we must have a creed, why not use "I confess" rather than "I believe"? "I confess" has the nuance of experience, of embracing something that is beyond categorization.)

I recently had an argument with a so-called Christian about the words faith and belief. He said to me, "*ya either got faith or ya got unbelief, and there ain't no neutral ground.*"[132] I angrily retorted, "there are only two types of people in the world: those who believe that there are only two types, and those who do not." More seriously, though, the thinking that one either has faith or has unbelief belief is painfully simplistic. It wrongly assumes that such words mean the same thing; but this is not at all the case. Whereas "belief" often stresses the existence of an outer reality, "faith" concerns the appropriation of that outer reality. Here is an analogy. I recently beheld a death-defying spectacle. A rope was suspended high above the length of the coliseum, and then a man with a long pole walked across it. The man then did so again, but this time his assistant was on his shoulders. An onlooker then said to the man, "Bravo! I believe that you could do it yet again." The performer replied, "Great. You believe; but do you have faith? If so, I will carry you rather than my assistant." We believe in things outside of us, but we have faith only when we trust, and we only trust as we are moving. If we stop walking because we want to analyze the tautness of the rope, we lose our balance and fall off. Even so, loving Jesus is not a matter of mouthing the right words: a test of my faith is not if I believe that Jesus died for me, but if I die daily for him—and as I participate in truth, I will daily say, "*It's not if I believe in Love, it's if Love believes in me.*"[133]

I also have a problem with how the word "righteousness" is bandied about. This word is principally about relational fidelity. Righteousness concerns strengthening a relationship by doing what is right. "If," this word implies, "you are in relationship with God, you will do what you can to prosper this relationship." Followers of Jesus are righteous because they live in his kingdom, which is an overflow of the goodness of God to the world. The righteous person, who is overcome by the mercy of God, loves because she has been loved.

Another lexical problem that I have with so-called Christians concerns their unreflective use of pronouns. Christians often make a careless distinction between "*I and You.*"[134] Rather than having a "what's in it for me?" attitude in which people say "*you for you and me for me,*" the Christian recognizes that every one of the multitudinous "I's" participates in God— the singular "You."[135] However disagreeable or unbelieving they might be, every "I" is suffused with the image of God; every "I" contains within itself a spark of the "You." Lost and forlorn though they might be, everyone is of infinite worth—simply because they bear within themselves the "You." "Whatever you did for others," Jesus said, "you did for me." All power-mongering is similarly based on the distinction between "us" and "them." It is only when this distinction is dissolved that "we" can be compassionate to "them" (insofar as "we" think of ourselves as being more special than "them," "we" can only think less of "them"). For those who live in the kingdom, there is never any room to think that "we" are somehow better or more deserving than "them," for we are all equal—even as Epimenides said of Zeus, "he is the father of us all."

The most troubling word that I have an issue with is how so-called Christians use the word "word." Many think of the word only as a synonym of scripture; but this understanding of the word "word" is itself most unscriptural—for more often than not the word "word" in scripture is a spoken word. The word is living and active, not the arrangement of a letters on a scroll. Creation came into being through a spoken word; the word of God "came to" prophets; and, most importantly, the Word of God became flesh. The Word of God, the Logos, is a person, not a book. Far from being just a matter of semantics, thinking of the Word of God as a book rather than the Son of God is idolatrous. (Such idolatry, however, is not identified as such because it is cloaked in supposed sacredness.) It is the Son of Man himself who mediates the love of God, not scrolls about the Son of Man. We "know about" the Son of Man from the scrolls, but we don't "know" the Son of Man from the scrolls—for the scrolls point beyond themselves to the Son of Man. If they had a voice, the scrolls would say, "Don't fixate on us, but on the One to whom we point."

Similar to the way that the word "word" is carelessly used, is how words concerning different virtues are used. Take "wisdom" as an example. The wisdom that the Christian seeks does not simply concern the practical application of knowledge. The Christian does not seek such wisdom but the very ground of wisdom, Wisdom himself. It is terribly short-sighted to think of Jesus simply as being extraordinarily wise, for he himself is Wisdom. So also, the Christian does not, technically speaking, strive for any one virtue but the ground of all virtue, which is none other than a person. This is even true of that one virtue that unites all the virtues together, the virtue of love, for the Christian does not simply want to be more loving, but to participate in Love.

(I here pause to think of the famed Socrates. Socrates did not believe the oracle at Delphi who said that he was the wisest of men. In order to prove her wrong, Socrates interviewed men who were reputed to be wise. He discovered that the oracle was right after all, that he was wise because he alone knew that he didn't know. He knew that fundamental to wisdom is a humility that says, "I don't know"—as such, Socrates was a pre-Christian Christian. The Christian sees such humility in the Logos, for the Son of Man became enfleshed Wisdom when he "emptied itself.")

You might be encouraged to know that while I dislike what so-called Christians say and think, I happily confess that I am sympathetic with Christian faith. (I am just not sure that "Christian faith" always accords with the teaching of Jesus.) Contrary to gnostic thinking, I am not at rest in making a divide between physical and spiritual reality. Implicit in the divine act of creation and in God becoming flesh is the centrality of the physical—the Spirit has chosen the material world as the conduit through which Love operates. Spiritual and physical realities unite in the Son of Man, the Logos. *I'll fly away* and leave this earth if, like the Son of Man, I bring heaven to earth in my life. I do not rejoice that there are *no more cold shackles on my feet*, for such shackles give me freedom.[136] The so-called "chains of physical existence" are, in fact, opportunities to grow in the freedom of the kingdom. Heaven is not, similarly, just some place that we go to when we die; but it is now, earthy, real. When faith is reduced to belief about metaphysical matters, it becomes unreal, not heaven at all. When, however, we do to others what we would have them do to us, we may be experiencing heaven: however faint it might be, we make *a heaven of hell*.[137] No, true believers will not waffle about in some nether region playing worship music because they thought the right way about things. No, *God is* not *watching us from a distance*,[138] for the Son of Man is *the ever-present man for others*.[139] Being in the Son's image, we will reflect him—such that people will say, "I experienced God as you loved me."

Vignette 24

Malchus and a Zealot

WHILE SIPPING HIS COFFEE, a Zealot argued with Malchus. The Zealot contended that might must be confronted with might. He then boasted of how he had killed a soldier.

"My aged father had been selling trinkets in Jerusalem. Early last summer, two Roman soldiers stopped at stall number 11, which was his. One of the soldiers reprimanded him: 'The items that you are selling were made by enemies of Rome. You must stop selling them immediately.' The next day my father was still hawking wares when the same soldiers came by. No sooner had my father greeted them, than one of the soldiers overturned the table—even as the other stood at the ready with his sword drawn. This latter soldier reproved my father: 'You are getting what you deserve, old man. Yesterday we told you to desist from selling your wares, but here you are still selling them. You cannot fool me, for I am cleverer than you: I can see through your duplicity—for while you greeted me, you inwardly despise both me and Rome.' My wife, who was at stall number 12, quickly ran to tell me what was happening. I became possessed by rage. What I did next was a blur, but I evidently rushed to the scene, wrestled the offending soldier to the ground, and slit his throat."

Malchus thought that he should say something, but the horror of what the Zealot recounted had left him speechless. The Zealot then continued.

"I have since had misgivings about why I murdered the soldier. I just said that slitting his throat was a blur; but the more that I ponder on it, the less hazy the blur becomes. I see that I was an accident waiting to happen, for years before the fateful episode I had given myself over to rage. The rage festered and grew, and then, like a life-denying serpent, it struck, and its venom has spread throughout my mind. I had become the very thing that I despise, and killing the soldier was only a consequence. While I still believe that might must be confronted with might, I must rise above might."

The Zealot then stopped to sip his coffee, and Malchus spoke.

"You are only thinking of yourself. You are stressed about your motivations; but what about the family and friends that the soldier has left behind? You are correct, however, in your assertion that you have become the very thing that you hate: *you became a monster so the monster would not break you*.[140] Some people think that they can defeat violence by being violent, but *kicking the darkness until it breathes daylight* will only make one's foot sore.[141] Using evil to overcome evil is akin to trying to dowse flames with oil. The answer to violence is not more violence but tough love—a love that *becomes the change that it wants to see* even as it longs to see such love in a world of strife.[142] The one who calls himself the Son of Man similarly says that peacemakers are blessed, for it is only the meek who will inherit the earth. Being meek is difficult in a world fueled by power, yet those who believe that one's commitment to goodness in this life will be extended in the next life rightly say that '*he is no fool who gives what he cannot keep to gain what he cannot lose*.'"[143]

Vignette 25

Morpheus, the Happy Taxpayer

WHILE LOUNGING IN HIS breezy courtyard and sipping a tasty beverage, Morpheus talked to his friend about the importance of maintaining the status quo (like his divine namesake, his chief interest was sleep).

"*Something is rotten in the state of Judea,*" Morpheus said to his friend as he sighed, "for many Judeans get offended when Jewish men collect taxes.[144] Their argument is that such men are implicitly supporting Rome; but even if this is the case, what's wrong with that? What they really should be asking is, 'How does this affect me?' I have also come to recognize that everyone has an angle—an ultimate concern through which every matter is evaluated. Rome's angle is that it wants all nations to submit to its power. Judea's angle is that it wants to be self-governed. My angle is myself. One's nationality is only an accident of birth; and I really don't care about who is leading the nation. *The only thing that really matters is what happens to me.*[145] Contrary to many folks, I think that Rome is doing a decent job; and I like living in *Happy Valley*.[146] My concern is not who rules the nation, but who gives me the most for the tax that I pay."

As Morpheus said this to his friend, he apologized for the odor that wafted into the courtyard. This was often the case when a breeze brought with it smells of decaying flesh—whether from sacrifices in the temple or from a recent spate of crucifixions. (Morpheus longed to move to a place free of troubles where he could relax—perhaps a wealthy oasis town with a spa in which he could soothe his tired bones.) Morpheus then invited his friend to recline in his living room.

After lumbering down the hallway, and then sitting down heavily on cushions in the living room, the friend said, "I concur with what you have said. Yes, he is a fool who gives to others what he can keep for himself; and yes, everyone has an angle. I recently heard a preacher from Galilee whose angle seems to be the derision of all angles, for, he said, 'It is not Rome or Judea that one should live for, but the Kingdom of God.' This is a politically shrewd stance, for at the same time that it discredits every angle, it sanctions an angle that nobody understands: everyone knows what Rome and Judea are, but no one knows what 'the Kingdom of God' is. Behind all this 'Kingdom of God' talk, there lurks the preacher's angle. Especially because he is a king without a kingdom, the preacher needs a following. Even as he stretched out on the cushions, Morpheus's friend continued his monologue. "I know the human heart. I know that what drives all people is selfishness. If the preacher gets his following, he will be satisfied—he might even think that this is a sign from the gods that he is doing the right thing. But make no mistake: his motivation is selfish. I don't have a problem with this—for I, too, am selfish!"

(While moving to the living room did manage to free him from the unpleasant smell, Morpheus concluded that the odor came from decaying humans hanging on crosses rather than from temple sacrifices. Confirming his thoughts were the unpleasant wails that accompanied the odor—which he likened to the sound of fingernails scratching a tablet. This conclusion was not a surprise to him, though: the Sabbath was approaching, and the soldiers removed corpses from crosses before it started—lest the crucifixions detract from rest.)

Morpheus was about to close the shutters of the living room window but he thought otherwise when his friend said that he would rather put up with the odor than sit in darkness. As with other important matters, Morpheus and his friend compromised: the shutters were closed half way (such that one could see in the dappled light a tired moth alight upon a web in a corner, only to become a living victim suspended between heaven and earth).

The conversation of Morpheus and his friend then moved to a recent controversy concerning the market. Some were saying that there should continue to be 12 stalls, while radicals were saying that there should now be 13. Morpheus said, "For years now, there have only been 12 stalls; we should not feel pressured by radical people who want to change the existing order and have 13 stalls." The friend, whose son-in-law wanted a stall in the market, was put-off by the insinuation that he himself was radical. His double-chin jiggled as he nervously guffawed: "Other marketers ought to make room for another stall. All the same, it may be that one of the 12 stalls has recently become free because of a needless ruckus between a soldier and a disturber of the peace."

Even as the controversy was brewing, the annoying smell continued to make its way through the partially closed shutters. Morpheus walked toward the window to close the shutters completely so that they could resume their important discussion. As Morpheus did so, he saw a man on the street with a bowl of water trying to give it to a criminal. Drops of sweat intermingled with blood trickled down the criminal's face and neck as he stumbled under the weight of a cross. Because the man refused to listen to a soldier who told him to desist from giving water to the parched criminal, the soldier rhetorically yelled, "*how many times can a man turn his head and pretend that he just doesn't see?*"[147] Morpheus at first thought that his friend was asking him this question because he was intent on closing the shutters, but he was comforted to know that it was only the soldier speaking. The whole matter reminded Morpheus that he needed to slake his own thirst; but because he wanted to treat his guest well, he first said, "Can I offer you another drink?" After Morpheus topped-off his friend's goblet that was resting on his protruding belly, he returned to the subject of the stalls. Morpheus slowly said, "I see your point. People need work. Perhaps, however, *the answer is blowin' in the wind*."[148]

(Morpheus thought that concurring with his friend while he himself closed the shutters would pacify his friend, such that his friend would overlook the closing. At the same time, Morpheus was careful to protect his own opinion—hence his statement that "the answer is blowin' in the wind." Morpheus similarly spoke slowly because he knew that doing so would further the friend's conviction that he, the friend, was right. More important than how many stalls there should be was maintaining civility: Morpheus even came to this conviction slowly, like a shadow incrementally moving on a sundial that is indifferent both to light and time—the very things that it is about.)

Knowing that his friend was enthralled with his own opinions, Morpheus continued: "What you said earlier about angles is true. Underlying all sacrifice is concern with self. Belief in God is also a selfish angle, for it concerns securing one's destiny." Pretending not to notice how his friend yawned, Morpheus carried on: "Just as everyone has an angle, so everyone is religious. No, not everyone goes to a sacred service, and not everyone is devoted to one god or another. What I mean by 'everyone is religious' is that everyone lives for something—whether it is money, fitness, family, or nation. The feelings are the same; all that differs is the object of the worship, such that one's *ultimate concern* is one's religion.[149] I really don't care what the preacher from Galilee says. I won't let that bastard grind me down, for his angle must not undermine my comfort. *I'm lookin' out for number one.*"[150]

Seeing that his friend agreed with what he was saying, Morpheus continued to prattle. "Various groups are passionate about their cause. One group calls itself 'Make Judea Great Again.' While many in this group say that they are devout, the truth is that they typically have little compassion. They are like their leader in this regard, who only pretends to be devout when doing so serves his Narcissistic impulsiveness. In my mind, 'Make Judea Great Again' is, nevertheless, on the right track. Its members understand that protecting self-interest is most important, and they will put up with any injustice toward others so long as their own comfort is protected. More specifically, 'Make Judea Great Again' is the best because it safeguards the tax that I pay. (The Romans have thoughtfully concluded that conquering 'shithole' countries leads to higher taxation.)"

Even as Morpheus said this, his chin bobbed up and down on his chest, for he was becoming drowsy. Morpheus's friend, whose eyelids were similarly becoming heavy, then nodded in agreement, wiped the perspiration that trickled down his forehead and puffy cheeks, and laboriously rose. The exhausted friend then thanked Morpheus for the pleasant afternoon and proceeded to leave. Morpheus was glad when his friend finally did so, for he could then fasten the shutters and sleep the rest of the afternoon away—which were proven strategies to escape odors of sacrifice. His sleep was fitful, though, for he did not know when he was awake or when he was asleep—even as he pondered on stalls.

Vignette 26

Forgiving Photis

A WOMAN NAMED PHOTIS had a wonderful life. While she did have a slight limp, her doting husband and her children helped her with troublesome tasks. Things had not always been so good for Photis, though, for her young years were horrible. For much of her life, Photis had been filled with anger at everyone, especially men. Such anger raised its head, and it would strike anyone who dared to come too close. It seemed to cast a shadow over everything that she said and did—even when she said that she was at peace, she said as much in an angry way. It was only when she started to attend the local synagogue that her life changed for the better.

While Photis was keenly interested in any subject that might assist her, she found that much of goodness comes together in the subject of forgiveness: when she thought about Sabbath rest, she at the same time said to herself, "I cannot be at rest so long as I harbour unforgiveness"; when she thought about faithfulness to her husband, she noted to herself that it is easier to be loyal when she forgives; and when she thought about the importance of tithing, she said that she happily supports the synagogue because her rabbi teaches how much God forgives.

Fundamental to her understanding of forgiveness was her growing conviction that she was no different than anyone else: the story of others was her story. Photis recognized that she participated in a common humanity; and she became aware that the hopes of others were similar to her own. Photis would say, "*I am he, as you are he, as you are me, and we are all together.*"[151] She would similarly say, "All compassion assumes that while everyone is special, no one is unique: *we are one, but we're not the same.*"[152]

Tied to this, Photis would say, "Being unable or unwilling to forgive is proportionate to how different or exceptional I think that I am."

Some synagogue members had heard that a preacher from Galilee would be in their environs within the week. Various authorities warned people about Jesus—saying that he neither upheld the scriptures nor the traditions of the elders. (The counsel of such authorities produced the opposite effect on people. "How," they reasoned, "could Jesus perform miracles if God was not with him?") Because she had no problem with challenging authority, Photis was one of the many who went to listen to Jesus. Much of Jesus' message, Photis happily noted, was tied to the subject of forgiveness. Photis particularly liked Jesus' statement to priests that "the prostitutes are entering the kingdom of heaven ahead of you." Photis similarly found comfort in the way that Jesus reprimanded religious leaders. "Go and learn what this means," he said: 'I desire mercy, not sacrifice.'" She liked these teachings because they concerned forgiveness.

Photis was both frustrated and elated when the subject of forgiveness came up at scripture studies. Photis became upset because she insisted on being practical (she knew that some who want to forgive are led astray by abstractions). For her, the subject of forgiveness was straightforward: it is simply wanting the best for those who had wronged her. An event happened at the synagogue in which the subject of forgiveness, she thought, was denuded of all mystification. On the night before a scripture study, a thief had stolen candle trimmers, an incense bowl, and other objects that could be melted down and sold (the scripture scrolls were much more valuable, but the thief left them). Soldiers captured the thief as he was clumsily pawning what he had stolen (he was missing one thumb). In desperation, the thief told the soldiers that the rabbi had given him the stolen items. The soldiers brought the thief to the synagogue, threw him to the floor, and jeeringly said that the thief had the audacity to claim that the rabbi had given the thief the items. Much to the shock of everyone, the rabbi said to the soldiers, "yes, I freely gave this man the items." But he then castigated the thief: "*why did you leave the most valuable item, the menorah*?"[153] The rabbi then gave the menorah to the thief, but as he did so, he whispered in his ear, "you owe your life to God."

When the thief freely left, the members returned to their study of forgiveness. Many of them seemed to think that God was merciful to them because they deserved it (they were, after all, good, upstanding people). In the days that followed, members recounted the episode, and they spoke about how the rabbi ought to have held the thief to account, how forgiving him taught him nothing, and how giving the thief the menorah dishonored those who gave their tithe.

Photis was exasperated. At the next scripture study, she said that mercy is present everywhere: it stays the hand of the wicked, it divides the darkness of humanity, and it is even present in Sheol. Photis then said that the congregants should celebrate the mercy given to the thief, and that maybe the mercy that he received would help him to embrace the kingdom—such that he, too, might become an instrument of mercy to others. Because the members did not seem to be cluing in, Photis reminded them that faith exhibits itself in mercy: "Micah declares that all that God requires is 'to do justly, to love mercy, and to walk humbly with God.'" Because some of the people appeared to be dismissive, Photis then became directly confrontational: "*You read the Bible in your special ways, you're fond of quoting certain things it says. Your mouth is full of righteousness and wrath from above, but when do we hear about forgiveness and love?*"[154] Quoting the prophet Isaiah, Photis similarly said, "all our righteousness is as filthy rags." Photis then caught herself: "If," she thought, "my friends don't understand mercy, it might be because they don't know how much they themselves have been forgiven."

One of the members in the synagogue, Mary Magdalene, confirmed what Photis was thinking. (It seems that Providence had brought Mary and Photis together to help each other.) Mary was concerned that while Photis understood mercy, she herself had not assimilated it. When the two of them were alone, Mary said to Photis, "Let God love you." Photis was unimpressed by this statement, so she answered, "What do you mean, 'Let God love you'? Of course God loves me. I know this is true." Mary then said, "Yes, God loves you, but the love of God is not only to be known about, it is to be experienced. Have you assimilated the love of God in your life?"

Mary then reminded Photis of how she started to understand mercy: "When I first understood forgiveness, I was overcome. I remember that I wiped and kissed Jesus' feet at the home of a highly respected Pharisee. This Pharisee thought to himself, 'righteous men must avoid wicked women.' Jesus then chastised the Pharisee: 'From the time that I came into your house, you did not give me water for my feet, but Mary has washed my feet with her tears; you did not give me a kiss, but Mary has not stopped kissing my feet; you did not soothe me with oil, but Mary has poured expensive perfume on my feet. Therefore, I tell you that her many sins have been forgiven, for she loves much; but he who has been forgiven little loves little.'" "When," Mary said, "we think ill of people because they don't understand mercy, we become judgmental like the Pharisee." Photis accepted Mary's quiet censure. It was as if God himself had spoken to her.

Vignette 27

Mary Magdalene

WHAT IS LOVE? WHEN asked what the most important commandment is, Jesus quoted Moses: "Love God with everything that you are; and love your neighbour as yourself." Jesus then said that everything in the scriptures is based on these two commandments. Love is what life is all about. God loves me, this I know, not only because the Bible tells me so, but because my heart tells me so. Love also includes feelings: even Moses said that we are to love with our "whole heart."

Yes, I love God. Saying that I want God is a painful understatement. I don't want God the way that I want good food or drink. Think of how a parched man under the desert sun longs for but a drop of water; this is how I long for God. I echo the psalmist's words: "As the deer pants for water, so my soul pants for you." I am beyond being enthralled. I pine for God, even as I depend on him, and even as I surrender my entire self to him in his goodness.

My favorite book in the scriptures is the Song of Songs. While at first it may have concerned passion between two lovers (even being erotic in places), it was later domesticated when it was thought to concern love shared between God and people. I concur with both interpretations, for there is but one love: like the union of Eros and Psyche, love between lovers is a reflection of ultimate Love. I pray with both perspectives when I say, "*that I may be chaste, ravish me.*"[155] My favorite service is, similarly, communion— which is often referred to as the love feast. "Feast" is the right word, for as I feed others, I myself am consumed by Love. The love feast is like a romance in which lovers woo each other. The chief difference is that the climax is not from Eros but from Agape—mercy received leading to mercy given.

I have been accused by my friends of being overly emotional. This accusation is not unfounded. The last time that I went to the amphitheater is a good example, for I was moved to tears by the tragic way in which the lovers did not come together. My friends were embarrassed by me. They were right: yes, it did not happen in reality; and yes, I knew the outcome. All the same, *I broke down like a little girl who could not hold back her tears.*[156] Even seeing children laugh or hug their mothers can make me weep—but with joy. I am filled with inexpressible thanksgiving when I see an old couple holding hands, or even when I smell a tiny flower. *Sometimes I see so much beauty in the world that my heart can't take it—at such times I feel that my heart is going to cave in.*[157] So also, when I look up into the sky on a starlit night my heart hears *the music of the eternal spheres.*[158] All creation is brimming over with praise. I cry out to God, "*You fill up my senses like a night in the forest, like the mountains in springtime, like a walk in the rain, like a storm in the desert, like a sleepy blue ocean. You fill up my senses, come fill me again.*"[159] The Spirit then replies, "*Come let me love you, let me give my life to you, let me drown in your laughter, let me die in your arms, let me lay down beside you, let me always be with you. Come let me love you. Come love me again.*"[160]

("Why," I ask myself, "cannot I be like others, like people who study?" I tried to learn to read like boys; but I gave up—not only because society frowns upon girls studying, but also because doing so bores me!)

Not unlike my friends, society has made its judgment: it accuses me of being flirtatious; but this is to misunderstand me altogether. Such accusations say more about society than about me. Society interprets reality through its own brokenness, only through the lens of passion. While society is darkly passionate, there is nothing wrong with passion itself. God himself *put into the composition of humanity more than a pound of passion to an ounce of reason.*[161] It is only when passion is self-centered that a problem arises: when one is passionate about oneself—one's accomplishments, abilities, or ability to reason. Society similarly associates purity with prudishness—but purity is to be defined by what it is, not by what it is not: purity is the ability to see every individual as a beautiful representation of God. When Jesus teaches about the kingdom of God, he is teaching about such beauty, *a beauty that will save the world.*[162]

One of my friends, who prides himself in his ability to reason, likens me to a butterfly, for, he jokingly says, I flit from flower to flower. According to him, I don't seem to be concerned with sustained thought. (All the same, he envies me. He wishes that tiny things in life could also bring him joy—tiny things like the flitting of a butterfly!) Even what I am now saying may not be "sustained." I don't care.

While the two of us were sitting beside a brook that was teeming with life, I asked my friend what sustained thought is. He said that conversation needs to have a logical progression—like the progression of numbers. He had evidently not assimilated his sustained thought, for the charming racket of a squirrel on a fragrant lilac tree then disturbed him. Making things worse, *a bird answered the squirrel in a pretty song*.[163] My friend then threw a stick towards *this tree by this brook* (towards as he said, "the noise and tangled brush"); but if he had listened carefully, he would have heard *the songbird singing that his thoughts were misleading*.[164] Upon finding himself again, he talked about syllogistic logic in which conclusions are necessary. . .

Premise one: all men are mortal;

Premise two: Socrates was a man;

Conclusion: therefore, Socrates was mortal.

While I don't dispute such reasoning, it seemed to me that the singing brook made more sense than his babble. To begin with, the "argument" presupposes that truth precisely accords with human reason—but *the most unreasonable thing is to think that everything is reasonable*.[165] So also, the use of the word "mortal" is terribly inappropriate, for being aware of one's own mortality has nothing whatever to do with reasoning. The use of this word is here telltale of a bankrupt understanding of what it means to be finite, what it means to *give birth astride a grave*.[166] (Aeneas rightly said that the burdens of mortality touch the heart infinitely more than they touch the mind.) So also, what is "a man"? A man feels, cares, fears, is distressed—and countless other emotions besides. (I feel sorry for people who say, "*Whereof one cannot speak, thereof one must be silent*"—such people evidently never heard someone say, "I love you").[167]

One day this friend brought me to a library. My pet dog accompanied us. My friend referred to the thousands of scrolls as a depository of truth; but I thought that the library was as ugly as Behemoth. My friend then spent hours perusing the scrolls and searching for truth in them; but I felt sad for him. The subject which all subjects will bow before is Love, and while my friend intuitively knew this, the pride that he entertained in his heart insisted that truth be coolly rational—just like him. My friend, who saw that I was miffed, then asked, "Why are you upset?" I impulsively replied, "My dog can see the scrolls, it can hear people reading them, but it cannot comprehend their contents. Similarly, *while you stand next to the truth, you can't see it; and even while truth is in your heart, you still won't believe it.*"[168] Adding insult to injury, I then took a mirror out of my bag and said, "You adore yourself, not truth, so here is a mirror." While what I said was altogether accurate, it was not kind. I apologized to him, but I don't feel that he likes me any longer, for I have not heard from him in some time.

Like my rational friend, other friends have wondered why I never married. They have said, "Given that Mary is so enthusiastic about relationships, it is odd that she is still single." My friends laughed at my response: "A woman needs a man like a fish needs a chariot," I said. More seriously, though, I am only interested in a relationship where I can love and be loved. (A man once tried to learn what love is through me, but his experiment was a disastrous failure—for neither he nor I knew the first thing about love.)

One sign of love is an ability to sense what a betrothed feels. The only man that I have had such chemistry with is Jesus, for it seems that he could intuit what I was feeling. I saw in him a beauty that is beyond physical description, such that I said to him, *"Lovin' you is so easy because you're so beautiful."*[169] I did say this, but my love for him cannot be compared to his love for me. *I really don't know how to reciprocate his love,* for it is all-consuming.[170] The love of Jesus is stronger than death and more passionate than the grave; it is *deep and vast like a mighty ocean, unmeasured, boundless, and free.*[171] While everyone wants to *drown in this sea of love,*[172] and while all love is but a whisper of this much greater love, largely because of *haunting memories that cling like sea urchins to our souls,*[173] we have only known it in part. I myself pray, *"Beauty, so ancient and so new, late have I loved you."*[174]

Vignette 28

Tyche and Jonathan

"Why," said Tyche to Jonathan, "is Jesus so opposed to wealth?"

"Jesus would be more successful," Tyche continued, "if he dispensed with his ideas about money: he likened the rich farmer who wanted to build bigger barns to a fool; he said that 'it is more possible for a camel to go through an eye of a needle than for a rich man to go to heaven'; and that 'one cannot serve both God and money.' If Jesus wants adherents, he should not use extreme language, for all people want to be rich."

"It is not," Jonathan answered, "that Jesus is opposed to wealth itself. I myself recently gave half of my money to the poor. If he was opposed to riches, Jesus would have said, 'this is not enough; you must give it all.' As it was, though, Jesus said, 'Today salvation has come to you.'"

Almost as if he wanted to reassure himself, Jonathan continued: "Jesus is not opposed to riches, but to the way in which people allow wealth to cloud what is important. You might recall a story in which a rich man asked Jesus what he must do to inherit eternal life, and in which Jesus said, 'Give everything that you have to the poor, then come, follow me.' The 'come, follow me' is important. The rich man could not follow, for he wanted himself more than he wanted God."

Looking for any hole, Tyche called attention to what she thought was inconsistent. "Why," Tyche said, "did Jesus tell the rich man that he had to give 'all' his wealth to the poor, but he was content when you only gave 'half' of your wealth?"

Jonathan responded: "Salvation is nuanced differently for every individual." Because he did not want to lose momentum, Jonathan continued:

"While Jesus tailor-makes salvation according to individual need, being generous is not an elective. The follower of Jesus cannot say, 'I believe, but I will not be generous.'"

Feeling threatened, Tyche protested: "*Don't give me that 'do goody-good' bullshit.*[175] Your words do not take into consideration different variables. If, for instance, the poor are undeserving, does it not follow that being generous is to encourage bad behavior? I know, for example, of beggars who only pretend to be needy. Generosity must be tempered by shrewdness. Perhaps, moreover, one can save and get interest and give all the more—by withholding funds one can be more generous."

Because she thought that she was on a roll, Tyche then candidly recounted an experience that she had had: "Years ago, when I was a cook in Caesar's army, I lived in a village that bordered a hostile nation. Whenever I emptied a clay vessel of its contents, rather than throwing the vessel away I set it down in the market—thinking that it would be useful to someone. On one such occasion, two respectable villagers fought over the vessel. I learned from this that the poor are as concerned about acquiring what they don't have as the rich are with protecting what they do have—rich and poor are equally materialistic."

Being frustrated by what he thought was apathy, Jonathan said, "We use excuses not to be generous—but that's just what they are, excuses. The truth is that we *don't give a flying fuck about the people in misery.*[176] Yes, we may be duped by an illegitimate beggar, or we might be generous in more productive ways, or the poor might be as materialistic as the rich—but none of these facts should dissuade us from being immediately generous. No doubt, while not being generous detracts from helping others, it also cripples us—for when we are not generous something within us dies. A core problem of not being generous is the insidious question, 'What's in it for me?' Such selfishness is a cancer to the soul, and the root of all evil." When we are not giving people, when we forever ask, 'What's in it for me?' it is because we do not understand that God has been generous to us. The prophet declares that this will change, for he teaches that in the last day 'the wealth of the nations will stream like a river' to the Messiah—in an act of worship, people will happily give back to God everything that they had received from God.

Assuming the role of a devoted Jew, Tyche then talked about the tithe: "Does not a prophet teach that one is to give ten percent to God? Surely that is generous."

Jonathan said, "Jesus has gone beyond earlier teachers; we are not required to give ten percent, but 100 percent. All that we possess is from God, and when we are generous we reflect how God has given himself to us."

Tyche again used pious thoughts to express herself: "If," she said, "God has granted me success in life, does it not follow that I should make as much as I can? Jesus said that not using my gifts is equivalent to burying my silver in the ground."

Jonathan said, "Yes, by all means, use your God-given abilities to make money, but then give it away as fast as you make it—for true *success is to give* as God has given."[177] Remember, also, that the amount that you give is not the same as generosity: the little that the widow put into the treasury was more than the vast sums that others gave. Like God, she gave of herself; *she gave until it hurt*."[178] The lovely irony here is that giving until it hurts produces yet more generosity—and therefore life.

Vignette 29

Nathaniel, the Trader

MY FATHER, WHO TRADED in distant lands, brought me on a journey. I was fascinated by many things, things that few people would ever behold: different peoples, the open sea—and yes, beautiful women. What captivated me most of all, though, were the different faiths of people and how faith shapes one's behaviour.

I first started to think about the relationship between faith and life when I met three beggars as I was helping to unload our ship: one beggar was a severely burned old woman, one was a crippled man, and one was a young deaf-mute. I say "met" rather generously; it might be more accurate to say that the beggars "accosted" me. They insisted on food or money, but all that I had was two gems.

(I call them "beggars" because that is how society speaks of them. As with most things, society opts for what is easy: it is easier to think of such people as bums who really ought to get a job than as equals who might need help.)

My father said that the deaf-mute was faking his malady. To prove his point, he dropped the iron tools that he was carrying. The tools clanged together, and the deaf-mute was startled. The sailors laughed at this, as did the two other beggars. To defend himself, the deaf-mute then made grunting noises. It turns out that his hearing was only impaired. I was then ashamed of my father. I ended up giving the deaf-mute one of my gems, and I gave the other to the burned woman; but both of them were ungrateful. This angered me, and I felt that it would have been better if I had not given them anything.

(Because the crippled man did not receive anything, I thought that he would be disgruntled, but he was not; he seemed to take it in as if being overlooked was part of his daily routine—but there was nothing routine about this whole experience for me.)

I have often reflected on this experience, for it typifies much of my life. I have learned that my life is tied to the needs of others. What is more, I have learned that we know little about the stories of others. (I learned, for instance, that the one man had been crippled by his parents in his infancy so that he might beg and earn money.) Related to such matters, I have learned that I can only love one person at a time. While I want to *throw my arms around the world*, I am frustrated because I am limited.[179] But my conscience says, "you can only love one person at a time" and that *you should not strive to do great things but little things with great love.*[180] A related matter concerns the difference between *loving humanity in general and loving the specific individual*.[181] It is relatively easy to help the needy world, but it takes grace to help the needy individual. The loving person will empathize, befriend, and seek to help the individual as if they themselves were in need. Another way in which the experience has shaped me is that it reminds me that we are all equal. I am no better than the beggars. As for showing them a better way, I must remember that this amounts to one beggar telling another where to find a stash of bread—for mercy has taught me that I, too, am hungry.

Even as I want to satiate the hungry, I remind myself that I must rest in my own hunger. As well-meaning as it might be, ceaseless introspection is devoid of mercy: I am loved simply because I am, not because of what I do or don't do. God's goodness to me does not depend on my righteousness to him, for if, as the saying goes, "we are faithless, he will remain faithful." Even making a choice to follow mercy is itself based on the goodness of God: living in the kingdom is not about deciding to choose love, but about allowing Love to choose oneself. All that one does is allow; no doubt, one must choose to allow—but that "choice" only amounts to a happy resignation that says "yes" to becoming aware that beauty is beckoning us, to wanting mercy to flow through oneself (like wine flowing out of a vessel which does not stop to ask how it might do so).

Vignette 30

Hallel, the Deaf-mute

I AM A DEAF-MUTE. Because I offended the gods, people have often been abusive. Children have been particularly cruel. It was not their sticks and stones that hurt me, but their cruel words (expressions speak volumes). Even adults, who ought to know better, have judged me.

Years ago, I found myself at a wharf without money or food. A man did not believe that I was truly deaf, so he made a loud clanging sound behind me. Because I can faintly hear, and because I felt vibrations, I was startled. Other beggars then laughed boisterously, for they assumed that I was only posing as a deaf-mute.

I then made my way from the wharf to the market. Upon arriving at the market, I gestured to a fruit-seller that I wanted to buy some produce. But the fruit-seller's attention moved from my grunts to an altercation in which several soldiers led a group of parched prisoners. The soldiers stopped at a well to refresh themselves, but they did not allow the prisoners to do likewise. Jesus, who was there at the time, gave one of the prisoners *a bowl of water*.[182] Upon seeing this, one of the soldiers shouted for Jesus to desist, but the prisoner had drunk some of the water. The prisoner dropped the bowl—in part, I assume, because he was missing a thumb. Jesus then turned from the altercation and noticed my uneasy situation. He placed his hands over my ears and said a short prayer. I was awakened to another world—one which I knew existed but had never experienced.

I desperately wanted to say "thank you" to Jesus, but because my tongue was untrained I could not enunciate the words. I didn't only want to say "thank you for healing me," but "*thank you for hearing me.*"[183] Prior to meeting Jesus, *I was silent, alone and without company*,[184] for people would unkindly say, *"your lips move, but I can't hear what you're saying."*[185] It was not just my expression that Jesus read, for he seemed to know my thoughts—even better than I myself knew them. Jesus knew that my heart was full of praise, that I was lost in wonder, that my heart said, *"amazing grace, how sweet the sound."*[186]

Now that I can hear, my problem is my speech—which rarely improves on silence. While I wanted Jesus "to train my mouth that my lips might proclaim God's praise," I have since learned that my speech is a windvane of my impure heart. Because, like me, people are not comfortable with their hearts, they despise silence; and so they *fill empty spaces* by making vacuous sounds.[187] Such discomfort is symptomatic of a diseased heart through which *people talk without speaking and hear without listening*.[188] They would rather use *silly chitter-chatter* than say one meaningful word (assuming that they knew what is meaningful).[189] While their conversation does an admirable job in masking thoughtless existence, it excretes only verbal diarrhea—which is as foul as it is insignificant.

Jesus loved silence. The noise in his life was proportionate to his need for silence. I surmise that such silence came out of his wisdom, a wisdom that he invited others to embrace. Jesus could say to those who were always thinking about what they might say: "make up your mind not to worry beforehand, for I will give you words and wisdom." Focus must not be on possible future circumstances, but on Jesus who gives present wisdom—and such wisdom is born in silence.

This is in accord with what we find in the scriptures. David could say, "I have quieted my soul." Elijah heard God not in the wind, the earthquake, or the fire, but in a quiet whisper. So also, the prophet could say, "in quietness and trust is your strength." The prophet similarly tells us that, unlike political aspirants, the messiah "will not shout or cry out or raise his voice in the streets" because God "will waken him morning by morning, will waken his ear to listen as one being taught." I also think of the psalm that says, "The heavens declare the glory of God, the skies proclaim the work of his hands; day after day they pour-forth speech"—even though the heavens and the skies are silent, they "declare" and "proclaim" the glory of God. It was in this *sound of silence* that Jesus found strength.[190]

I learned more about silence as I witnessed the sentencing of Jesus. (The word "trial" is a misnomer: even before evidence was heard everyone shouted, "crucify him.") Whether the accusation came from Herod, Pilate, or religious leaders, Jesus rarely spoke—in part, because he speaks a different language. The silence of Jesus amounted to an answer-less answer, for his silence proclaimed the truth. At one point during the sentencing, Pilate asked Jesus, "What is truth?" Jesus remained silent. I myself was hoping that Jesus would seize this opportunity to speak. Some say that Jesus was silent at this point because he was a sacrificial lamb. They use Isaiah in support of this view: "he was led like a lamb to the slaughter, and as a sheep before its shearers is silent, so he did not open his mouth." But I can't agree with this interpretation, for anyone who has seen a lamb being sacrificed will hear its loud bleating. I think that the silence of Jesus was more akin to what Amos said. In light of the horrible suffering that they witnessed, Amos commanded the people to be silent—for in the face of injustice and suffering, words have no meaning.

Jesus was an echo of God, and insofar as echoes reverberate through silence, for those who have ears to hear, the reverberation is pleasantly deafening. To hear that reverberation, I need to become deaf to the echoes of meaningless chitter-chatter—and so be healed of empty speech.

Vignette 31

Barabbas and Hamaeus, the Criminals

ELIHU ENTHUSIASTICALLY CHANTED THE psalm with other synagogue members; but his voice quaked when he intoned, "Why do the righteous suffer?"

Every Sabbath was the same. In the afternoon, some of the congregants would go to the prison to lead a worship service and help the inmates—cutting their hair, dressing their festering wounds, or giving them food. Two of the inmates who refused to come to the service were chained to a common wall. One was Barabbas, the son of Elihu. The other was named Hamaeus, whose distinguishing mark was a missing thumb. Barabbas had asked Hamaeus how he had lost his thumb. Hamaeus told him that while he was fleeing from a robbery a soldier struck him with a sword. He said that he seized the sword from the soldier and then killed him. (The truth, though, is that Hamaeus lost his thumb when he clumsily got it pinched between his chains and the chains of another prisoner during a scuffle over a stale bread crust.)

Prison had been horrible for both of them. The guards were angry when Barabbas came to the prison because there were no empty walls upon which he might be chained. Barabbas then said something abusive to them. To teach him to be more respectful, the guards chained his wrists to his ankles in the hot sun with no food or water, and forced him to wallow in his own waste for the day. As for Hamaeus, he had stolen a chicken. The people who caught him stripped him of his tunic, put a collar on him that had six holes in it with ropes in each hole, and then dragged and jerked him through the streets—even as onlookers pelted him with refuse. Neither

Barabbas nor Hamaeus, however, told the truth to each other about why they were in prison, for doing so would have detracted from their honor.

While they did enjoy the company of each other, Barabbas became increasingly frustrated over how Hamaeus used his defecation pot. Rather than urinating on the inside wall of the pot, Hamaeus aimed for the center—making a terrible gurgling sound for all those in earshot. Hamaeus was also in the habit of leaving the pot on a slight slope. The end of his chain marked the beginning of this slope, and he naturally placed the pot as far away as possible so that the stench would not assault him. The problem is that the pot sometimes tipped over at the base of the slope, spilling its contents and making the air more putrid than Augean stables. All of this, Barabbas thought, was terribly selfish. For his part, Hamaeus became increasingly agitated over how Barabbas continually played with his chains. Barabbas delighted in making different shapes with his chains: he divided the chain into four equal lengths and laid them out to make a square; and he used similar reasoning to make other shapes—including connected circles. He then framed his masterpieces by etching borders in the dirt and rock—all the while being careful not to upset his pot. While Hamaeus was initially impressed by what Barabbas did (it brought a measure of beauty to the putrid cave), the clinking sound became an irritant. What angered Hamaeus most of all was the seeming disregard that Barabbas had of others. Hamaeus saw in the action of Barabbas untold selfishness, which made him want to urinate in his pot all the more loudly, and he also set the pot closer to Barabbas so that the odor would waft toward him. This, he thought, was one way of getting even.

The irritations of both Barabbas and Hamaeus had a welcome reprieve when the guards scored several flasks of wine. Because the wine was sour, and therefore unfit for human consumption, they gladly gave it to the prisoners (seeing the prisoners get drunk would make their shift entertaining). In his drunkenness, Barabbas told Hamaeus that the occasion reminded him of how he had secretly fermented grapes in his father's vineyard. Barabbas also told Hamaeus a story that was not so savory: one day after he had drunk much of the wine that he had made, he passed out and lay naked in a lean-to, and his uncle raped him. As Barabbas recounted the episode, he shook uncontrollably. Hamaeus initially thought that Bacchus had possessed Barabbas in an ecstatic blend of drunkenness and frenzy; but far from ecstasy, the shaking was from pent-up anger. Barabbas said, "He gave me a name that means 'son of the father.' What gall! If he really was a father, he would have protected me. He ought to have known what his brother might do. That is why I will not talk to him." After he sobered up, Barabbas did not remember what he had told Hamaeus.

One Sabbath morning, Hamaeus overheard bits of the rabbi's homily. The rabbi said that people often defeat us not by anything that they do, but by how we think about what they may be thinking. "When we think about what others do or don't do," the rabbi said, "we are like a pig that wallows in its waste." "I am not," mused Hamaeus, "a pig that wallows in waste." He humbly but stridently said to himself, "*no man is my enemy, for my own hands imprisoned me.*"[191] The rabbi similarly said that a secret of inner-peace is to learn to love what one often hates. Hamaeus contemplated yet more upon what the rabbi had said, such that he even forced himself to enjoy the way that Barabbas clinked his chains. While initially the sound grated on him, he later grew indifferent to it; and, from time to time, he almost enjoyed it—as if Barabbas was using *prayer beads* in worship.[192] Hamaeus concluded that what is most important is not the tinkling, but how he thought about the tinkling.

Hamaeus came to a similar conclusion when he and Barabbas argued about who has the more enviable position—the prisoner who defecates in the pot or the slave who cleans out the pot. Barabbas contended that the prisoner is in a more honorable position. In support of his argument, he asserted that the prisoner will one day be free, and that scooping out the waste of another is as low as one can get. Hamaeus disagreed, contending that waste, like the grave, makes everyone equal. "There is no difference," he said, "between the shit of a prisoner and the shit of a master." Hamaeus also sagely said that neither the prisoner nor the slave is in a more enviable position, for it is not circumstances that enslave people but how circumstances are interpreted: the freeman, while his circumstances may be wonderful, might be enslaved to his passions; and the slave, while his circumstances might be horrible, might be free in his heart.

The change in Hamaeus was slow, even imperceptible. Hamaeus first noticed that his thinking was changing with the tinkling; but as he reflected more on the matter, he thought that the change started when a rabbi had said to him years earlier, "you forgot the menorah." A new outlook had been dawning on him. "*Something happened, and somebody touched me, making everything new,*" he would say.[193] "*I'm thinking about eternity, some kind of ecstasy has got a hold on me,*" he would continue.[194] The change again struck Hamaeus when he and Barabbas *watched a guard savagely beat another prisoner.*[195] While they both said that they felt pity, they meant different things: Barabbas felt pity for the prisoner who was being beaten, but Hamaeus felt pity for the guard who was doing the beating. "The violence within the beater," Hamaeus said, "comes from his own horror."

A short time after the beating, Elihu, the father of Barabbas, learned that Hamaeus was about to be released. Because he needed more help, Hamaeus consented to a job offer from Elihu that involved working in his vineyard. One day, while Elihu's rabbi was pruning alongside Elihu, Hamaeus overheard their conversation.

Elihu said to his rabbi, "Why did Barabbas turn out this way? I don't understand. I have been a righteous father. I trained him in the way that he should go, yet he turned from it, and he has brought much suffering to me." Rather than answering immediately, the rabbi continued to listen—even as Elihu sobbed: "Barabbas, you are my only son; it is you whom I love." The rabbi then set down his pruning fork and said, "You have not done anything wrong. Barabbas has his reasons for hating you—even if you don't know them, or even if they are illegitimate." Elihu wept all the more: "O my son Barabbas, my son, my son. Worse than anything that you have done is the fact that you won't talk to me, and I don't know why." The rabbi was lost for words. He then prayed, and said things that he himself was surprised by: he knew that much of what he said was already known to Elihu, but he did not know that what he said was also for eavesdropping Hamaeus. The rabbi said, "This is not *the best of all possible worlds.*[196] People who say as much are often like Job's friends, for they declare that suffering exists because of sin. This is a frightful oversight, for innocent people suffer as much as wicked people. Yet suffering reveals truth even as it itself is beyond understanding. The same occurrence makes its way through different people's lives in diverse ways. Hashem seamlessly weaves together people and circumstances. Remember what Joseph said to his murderous brothers: 'You meant it for evil, but Hashem meant it for good.' Rather than trying to explain suffering, we must learn to embrace it, to say, 'I don't know why this is happening, but I don't need to know; I must trust.'"

Years later, while Hamaeus was in Jerusalem, he was with the crowds who shouted for the release of the son of the father and the crucifixion of the Son of Man, but, unlike them, he struggled with who ought to be released—even as he reflected that *God sees the truth but waits.*[197]

Vignette 32

Daniel, the Righteous Judge

AFTER THE JUDGE COMBED his mustache, he went to bed. As he was falling asleep, he thought, "I am proud of what I do. I protect society from evil people."

"Not long ago," the judge mused, "I tried a man who had stolen a chicken. The trial was a masquerade, for I knew that I was going to find him guilty. My reason was simple: he had a record of committing crimes, including murder and sedition. People feared to report his theft, for upon release the prisoner might avenge himself. When I sentenced the thief, wise man that I am, I warned him that if anything should happen to the accusers, I would have him tortured. 'If anything,' I told the thief, 'you ought to protect the family.' Many months later, I learned that the accuser had been murdered. It infuriated me that the criminal had not taken my warnings seriously, and I immediately had him apprehended."

"I instructed the soldiers to keep the criminal at the back of the courtroom while I asked him mandatory questions, for allowing him to be close to me was to recognize him as human—but he was more like a rabid dog that needed to be put down. I then shouted at the criminal, '*In all my years of judging I have never heard before of someone more deserving of the full penalty of law. The way you made the family suffer fills me with an urge to defecate.*'[198] The murderer was then forcibly brought before me to receive his sentence; but I was then filled with foreboding, for I recognized his face as my own—I was judging myself even as I judged him."

"I then awoke. It had been a nightmare. While I was drenched in sweat and trembling, I was relieved to know that I was safely in my own bed.

My lovely wife sought to console me. Before going back to sleep, she said, 'Everyone thinks highly of you.'"

"As I reflected more on the dream in subsequent days, it occurred to me that *it didn't matter if it was a nightmare or reality*, for I, too, am a weak human.[199] The judgments I make in court," I thought, "are consistent with the judgments that I make in everyday life. Today, while I was in the market, I caught myself judging. 'That woman is too fat,' I thought, 'that one is full of rage, that mentally challenged boy understands nothing, that man observes others like a voyeur, that man has a gait that says, "I am self-made"—and those thieving boys may well appear before me.' I then asked myself, 'Who am I to judge? I don't know what their stories are. The motivations of their hearts are unknown. I don't even know my own motivations. Only God knows my heart, which *has become a restless inn, full of rumors*.[200] I myself am guilty, for I have cheated on my wife. How, then, can I judge others?'"

"My fellow judges (whose names are Rhadamanthus, Aeacus, and Minos) now think that I am unfit to judge, for they say that I have softened on crime. 'No one,' I would tell them, '*is fit to judge a criminal until he recognizes that he is such a criminal himself*.'[201] Their complaint is not true. It's not crime that I have softened on; it's others that I have started to understand—and as I do so I understand myself. '*We are all painted with the same brush*,' I would say."[202]

"My beautiful wife wants the old me back; but there is no going back. 'Only the messiah will judge perfectly,' I would say to her, for the prophet declares that 'he will not judge by what he sees, or decide by what he hears.'"

"Last month I heard a preacher from Galilee. The one thing that he said that I understood was about judgment. He said, 'Do not judge, or you too will be judged.' 'Why,' he asked, 'do you look at the dust in another's eye, but pay no attention to the beam in your own?' The crowd laughed at this analogy, but they did so nervously."

"This preacher evidently upset the establishment, for he has recently been imprisoned. I do hope, for his sake, that Brutus and Cassius are not guarding him, for they mercilessly rape prisoners before they are tried. I don't know which of my colleagues will judge the preacher. I am only glad that I will not have to judge him—for that would amount to me judging the Judge."

Vignette 33

A Converted Farmer

A FARMER, WHO LIVED at the base of Mount Nysa from which four rivers flow, took his donkey from its pasture and rode toward his vineyard. The farmer said to himself, "Because I love my vineyard, which I inherited from my adopted father, some have suggested that I am more suited to the worship of Gaia than the God of my fathers. What such people fail to understand is that love of creation is one with love of humanity. The two go together like a hand in a glove: one cannot be the keeper of one's brother if one does not also tend the garden." Upon reaching the vineyard, the farmer dismounted from his donkey. As he planted his calloused soles on the ground, it was as though the ground had arisen to meet them.

The farmer then tethered his donkey to a choice vine. (He knew that the donkey would happily eat the grapes, but grapes were abundant.) "The garden," he thought to himself, "will again be lush and verdant; but this will not happen until the Seed of the Woman comes. This messiah will cultivate gently, for the prophet teaches that 'a bruised reed he will not break.' This same prophet refers to the messiah as 'a shoot' and 'a branch' who will bring in everlasting righteousness to the world."

As the farmer mulched pig dung into the soil, he continued to muse. "There was a time that I did whatever I could to escape the odor of waste. I have since learned that things that are loathed can be instruments of life."

As the farmer grafted a fruitful vine onto one that was less fruitful, he was filled with quiet joy. He then massaged his gnarled fingers, which were so dirt-stained that it would be not be a wonder if a sprig came up in the place of his missing thumb.

"The scriptures teach," the farmer reflected, "that there is a relationship between the righteousness of humanity and the health of creation. The end will be like the beginning: when humanity becomes itself, the garden will again cover the earth. Right now, however, wickedness abounds: *trees are ablaze in the promised land*—even as people *hack, burn, and pave paradise* to make things better for themselves.[203] All the same, people will one day realize that *grapevines have unnecessarily been cut down*[204] because of universal selfishness: *it's a wonder, indeed, that more trees aren't laying down—for even when I was boy we'd tear trees down and use them on our enemies.*"[205]

As the farmer then led his donkey to the barn, he reflected on current events. "The one who calls himself the Son of Man will soon be crucified. Only a humanity that is as twisted as a vine," the farmer continued, "could invent crucifixion: people lop branches off a living tree and affix a dead cross-member to it. This is so contrary to the torah: Moses commanded Israel not to destroy trees; and while he said that anyone who is hung on a tree is cursed by God, blessings may nevertheless come from this curse." I hope that his tree will be one of the last to fall before the garden is again lush.

As the farmer removed the burden from the donkey, he himself was reminded of a great weight that had come off him. Living in the garden was beyond anything that he could have dreamed, for he knew that his adopted father wanted to give it to his estranged son. The farmer then reminded himself that his freedom was tied to the happy imprisonment of owing his life to God, even as he prayed, "*let thy goodness like a fetter bind my wandering heart to thee.*"[206] His rejoicing was greater than that of the harvesters when new wine abounds.

Vignette 34

Simon of Cyrene

"HEY YOU," THE SOLDIER yelled. "No, not you. The black one. Yes, you! Help this filth."

I helped Jesus stand; but his legs buckled under the weight. On any other day it would have been easy for him to carry the cross; but this was not an ordinary day.

Jesus probably had had a horrid experience in the prison: perhaps being mocked and spat upon—but still offering his back to those who beat him and his cheeks to those who pulled out his beard. The guards put a purple robe on him, and they placed a crown upon him, but only to mock him—for he said that he was a king (the crown itself was not bedecked with jewels, but was a woven thorn bush).

I hate and love the cross at the same time.

I hate the cross, because it compromises my need to be admired. Like a gadfly that forever pesters me, the cross is an irritant that reminds me that I live for myself.

When I first started making crosses, I thought that doing so would be easy money; but making crosses was more difficult than I had thought. The soldier in charge gruffly told me that I must be sure to smoothen the wood of knots (if the crosses were not smooth, I might find myself on one such cross myself). With the first crosses that I made, I tried to lop off the knots. Every time that I missed the base of the knot, I ended up having to smooth the indentation that the hatchet made—thus making more work for myself.

As I helped Jesus carry the cross, I immediately recognized it as one that I myself had made—for the scars left from the hatchet were plainly visible. When I first carried the cross, I managed to get a painful sliver under my thumb nail, which produced a constant throbbing. I had gone a short distance when I also felt a knot jabbing into my shoulder blade. If I avoided the knot by adjusting the weight of the cross, then the sliver in my thumb produced more pain. I found that the best thing to do was to squeeze the knuckle of my thumb with any available finger. Doing so kept the throbbing of my thumb to a minimum, even as it kept my mind from fixating on the knot that was jabbing into my shoulder blade. I lamented to myself: "*Jesus Christ that hurts!*[207] Couldn't they have found wood that was less knotty?" Had I known that I was making the cross that I myself would carry, I would have made it differently. I would have used lighter wood. I would have removed the rough edges, and I would have carved it to match the contours of my neck and shoulders.

Jesus then stumbled from exhaustion. As he did so, the crown of thorns that he was wearing pierced through his flesh to his skull. At this point a man with a missing thumb *tried to give Jesus some water* so that Jesus could slake his thirst and wipe his brow; but before the man could do so a soldier flogged him.[208] While I appreciated the man's attempt, he brought me further discomfort, and the whole matter was painfully inconvenient. Worse than the gadfly that buzzed around my head and bit into my flesh, carrying the cross interrupted my day—and it made me look like I was in need of mercy.

I thus hate the cross; but I also love the cross because the death that it brings is life-giving. I know that *dying to myself is to live.*[209] I have learned that the more that I live for myself, the less happy that I am. I must, therefore, have a holy selfishness in which *I crucify my mind and commit the sin of envy whenever I hear the story of the cross.*[210]

Which am I to choose? Hatred of the cross or love of the cross? This question is like a *sliver in my mind* that is always before me.[211] The question of hating or loving the cross accords with the fact that *Christ's cross and Adam's tree stood in the same place.*[212] My answer is not one or the other. It is, rather, a unhappy commingling of the two. I would not be human if I did not want what is best for me, so I hate the cross; and I would not be what I want to be if I did not crucify my selfishness. My choice, therefore, is both hate and love.

An enemy of love of the cross, can be, ironically, the very scriptures that concern the crucifixion—for while the scriptures may describe the story, they must not eclipse the daily experience of the story. As I carry the cross, I say to myself, "The story of Abraham's near-sacrifice of Isaac fore-shadows the crucifixion, for in each instance we read that a father sacrifices his innocent son in the mountains of Moriah. In both accounts, the son is puzzled. Isaac said to Abraham, 'The fire and the wood are here, but where is the lamb for the burnt offering?' Isaac was clueless. He didn't know that he himself was to be the lamb. So also, while Jesus knew that he was going to be sacrificed, he did not know why things had to happen in the way that they did. It would, however, be trite only to say that in both accounts 'the son is puzzled'—for the willing victims were ridden with fear and confusion: Isaac's despair came to a climax when his father raised the knife to slit his throat; and the despair of Jesus is heard in his cry: 'My God, my God, why have you forsaken me?' What were the two of them experiencing just prior to their demise? Issac said, 'I am bound. The blade glistens in the sun.' Jesus groaned, 'They throw me on the cross. The hammer gleams.' Adding to their pain, they both despaired: Why? Why?' But even in their despair, they trusted—as if the glistening and gleaming reminded them that God was with them: Isaac remembered that Abraham had told the servant, 'wait here until I and my son return from worshiping'; and Jesus recalled his father saying, 'after your suffering, you will see the light of life.'" My real experience of living then rudely interrupted my scripture reflection—for the throbbing of my thumb was again excruciating. "It is delightful," I said to myself, "to meditate on scripture, but reflection of the past must work itself out right now."

I have learned that time collapses in on itself in the cross: the past and the future together merge into the present, making the now eternal. While the crucifixion of Jesus happened in the past, the cross exists outside of time, for it is always before me. Every day I confess that *I was there when they crucified my Lord.*[213] Every day I assimilate what happened back then to what is happening now. Every day, I acknowledge that *I held the scabbard when the soldier drew his sword*, that I myself pounded the spikes, and that I need that mercy which I myself crucify.[214] Insofar as this does not happen, I crucify the cross—for the one who had life outside of time was crucified in time so that those in time might have life outside of time.

Vignette 35

Mary, the Disciple of Jesus

BETWEEN HER SOBS, MARY thanked Jesus.

"In the past, people referred to me as 'the woman from Magdala' for I was despised; but now they call me 'Mary Magdalene, the disciple of Jesus.' I was once just a slab of meat, but I have since learned that *it isn't to the palace that the Christ child comes, but to shepherds and street people, hookers, and bums.*[215] You taught me that love and forgiveness are inseparable, that there can be no love where there is no forgiveness. Help me, dear Jesus, to know how much I have been forgiven so that I might love. You taught me that the way that God forgives me is the way that I must forgive others. I must want the best for everyone—especially for those who have hurt me."

At this, Jesus looked at those who were jeering. Rather than repaying evil with evil, he prayed: "Father, forgive them, for they don't know what they are doing."

"You taught me," Mary continued, "that those who follow you may well be resented by others, but they themselves must never think ill of others. You taught me that people do wrong because they don't know any better. One week ago the crowds had shouted, 'hosanna, hosanna,' but today the same crowds shouted, 'crucify him, crucify him.' You nevertheless have had compassion on the crowd, for they are helpless; you even sought to protect them—like a hen protects its chicks. *The crowd is untruth*, and insofar as I want to follow you, I will explore every aspect of love and turn from what the crowd says (but as I do so I will watch my attitude, for if I condemn the crowd, I am no different than it)."[216]

MARY, THE DISCIPLE OF JESUS

Mary Magdalene then buried her face in her tunic; but before doing so she noticed the pain of Mary, the mother of Jesus—it's as if a sword had pierced her heart. Mary Magdalene then said to Mary, "At one time I mocked you, but now I know that the Lord will be with you as you cope with your pain, for you are full of grace."

I have also tasted the grace that nurtures you. As I look back on my life, I see that such grace has gently but certainly brought me to greater love. Before I came to you, *I only loved myself for the sake of myself.* But when, because of you, I came to you, things changed. *I then loved you not for who you are, but only for myself.* At times I participate in a greater love, a love in which my love of self is wed to love of God. Alas, however, I only taste of such love now and then. My journey toward this love is, thus, *not a victory march but a cold and broken hallelujah,* for I am haunted by gruesome memories.[217] I hope that one day I will forget such horror and bask in your mercy, that I will be so consumed by Love that self will no longer be in the equation. I will then confess that God, for whom all exists, is over all, and through all, and in all, and *I will then love you for your sake.*[218]

Jesus then said to his mother, "John is now your son," and to John he said, "my mother is now your mother." Mary Magadalene knew that this was in fulfillment of the teaching of Jesus that the world would know his followers by the love that they had for each other; and it was she who passed this story on at the love feast.

Vignette 36

The Roman Centurion

MY BLOOD-LINE WAS SUPERB. I came from a long line of heroes: my great-grandfather gave his life for the Empire at Actium, my grandfather was killed by northern hordes, and my own father died for Rome here in Jerusalem. I think, though, that the impressive pedigree will not continue. I used to justify killing, saying that Rome ought to impose its peace on godless people; but then I started to think that the brutality of Rome's peace is as dark as any godlessness. "I am sure," I said to myself, "that, just like Roman citizens love their children, the masses of people in foreign nations *love their children, too* (the only difference between the Empire and foreign nations is that Rome has greater power)."[219] As the years passed, I began to recognize that there is a peace that effortlessly works through Roman peace and the godless hordes, a peace that *will not kill the children anymore.*[220] I now despise the idea of trying to further my violent blood-line. "*Who are these men of 'guts,' greed, and glory?*" I ask myself.[221]

I was thinking this way when I met with my father at an inn. If truth be told, my father died in the service of violence, not of peace. Indeed, he lived in a world of violence that depends on other violence to sustain itself, for his throat was slit by a Zealot who opposed Roman rule. While we were at the inn, my father confessed as much. He told me that, years earlier, when he was stationed at a tiny outpost of Jerusalem, he had raped a Jewish girl. As is often the case with violence, rather than blaming himself, my father blamed the victim: "she was in the wrong place at the wrong time," my father angrily said before he belched.

Wanting to change the subject, I then told my father of a recurring dream. In my dream, after mingling with my own blood, a criminal's blood trickles from his heal to a puddle. The pooled blood then drains into a stream, which empties into the River Lethe, which itself converges with the *River Eunoe* before emptying into a sea that borders every nation.[222] My father discounted the dream by pointing out that the trickle of blood would make its way from Jerusalem downward to the bowels of the earth, the Dead Sea—not upward to the Great Sea. I should have known better than telling him my dream. ("How," I asked myself, "could good blood come from such bad blood?") Others have said that he was gutsy, but in truth he was *a man without a chest*—an unfeeling and wooden literalist who worships at the shrine of consistency.[223] For those with eyes to see, all existence is imbued with the divine, even as it portends that there is no distinction between the sacred and the secular: all alike is holy.

That night, I again had the recurring dream. The next morning, I was told that my duty for the day was to oversee the crucifixion of Jesus. Jesus was regarded as an enemy of peace, so I comforted myself in thinking that my job would be easy enough.

As Jesus staggered under the weight of the timber that he was carrying, he reminded me of my drunken little brother: not just because both of them staggered, but because they looked alike. I then yelled at a bystander, commanding him to assist the filth (yelling made my head throb as I had a hangover). The bystander did so; but Jesus again stumbled. Another man then attempted to give Jesus some water to drink—but the bowl fell out of his hands. When Jesus at long last made it to the hill upon which he was to be crucified, I had thought that it was essentially over. I only had to crucify the poor bastard, and then I could go home, eat, get drunk, enjoy my wife, sleep, and begin another purposeful day.

All that I had to do was maintain the peace. Doing so was straightforward. There was one scuffle between a soldier and a follower of Jesus, but nothing that a drawn sword could not squelch. There was also a heated argument between two other suspended criminals. (I let the squabble carry on, for I knew from experience that bickering would hasten their demise.) Another little problem was the mother of Jesus. She pleaded with me to give her son some water. Because I had learned that it is best to placate adversaries rather than infuriate them all the more, I told the soldiers to give Jesus water—consistent with his royal status, though, they mockingly gave him wine.

(When the mother pleaded with me through her teary eyes, she asked, "Don't I know you?" While I denied this, there was something within me that nevertheless said that we were one.)

I had seen it all before: the squabbling of other criminals, pleading for a drink, and the hovering birds of carrion looking for their next meal. What was different, though, was the last word of Jesus. While the sweat of his brow mingled with his blood, he said, "It is finished." Others thought that such words only pertained to his demise, but I divined that they meant more: as the words were uttered the sky became uncharacteristically dark, and the earth itself trembled. Like my recurring dream, such events were signs and portents.

No longer did I think of Jesus as a poor bastard, but as my brother (and, therefore, the Son of Man). I was crucifying my own brother, and I could hear his blood crying out to me from the cross. I then fell to my knees and said, "Truly, Jesus is the Son of God." It was here that I had an epiphany, that I became aware that beauty works through ugliness. All the same, it took some time before I was transformed, for most of existence was still standard: after my confession, I went home, I ate, got drunk, and enjoyed my wife, but the normal was suffused with the abnormal. I began to change. I eventually became a Christian.

Christians have asked me just what I meant when I confessed that Jesus is the Son of God. "In what sense," they ask, "is Jesus human, and in what sense is he divine?" They are often disappointed when I tell them that my confession was produced more from wonder than from careful thinking. The Son of God is beyond words and ideas. All that we can use is metaphor. The union of the divine and the human in Jesus is akin to intertwining melodies in a single score—the beauty of which is how such differing melodies produce harmony even as they blend. The paradox may also be likened to the relationship between iron and coals in a furnace: while the one who smelts iron knows that there is a difference between the iron and the coals, from his perspective it looks as though the two are one. This paradox is not so much to be puzzled over as it is to be embraced as a truth that creates humility—even as we Christians sing: the one who was in the "form of God" emptied himself by taking on the "form of a slave." I must do likewise: crucified to vainglorious pedigree, only to be resurrected to joyous new life. As individuals and nations are submerged in the rivers of mercy, they, too, will forget offenses and revel in goodness—thereby creating *something beautiful for God*.[224] When I confess that Jesus is the Son of God, this is what I mean.

Vignette 37

Judas Iscariot

I FIRST SAID TO myself, "Jesus may be a man who expresses my ideal." I later learned, however, that I was wrong. Ideals are solid and unchanging; but like John the Baptist before him, Jesus did not even know who he was. How, then, could he be an ideal?

When people expressly asked Jesus if he was the Christ, Jesus never said "yes" or "no." Some of his followers have said that Jesus did not want to encourage misguided expectations, and that Jesus therefore referred to himself as the "Son of Man"—a title that few understand. The fact is, however, Jesus simply didn't know who he was! He did not live up to the Greek maxim, "know yourself." This accords with the fact that Jesus was ignorant: he said, "even the Son of Man does not know when he will return." I have similarly been told that in his last breath he even asked God a question: "My God, my God, why have you forsaken me?" Jesus asked because he did not know.

Truth exhibits itself in an ideal, and ideals are, by definition, both certain and flawless. I first started to follow Jesus because I thought that he would deliverer Israel; but when he did not meet this ideal, I became lukewarm. I therefore took a position as his follower that I thought would demand the least amount of commitment. I decided to become the keeper of the money bag. My first priority was to make sure that we had enough money. Jesus taught us to pray "give us this day our daily bread" as if we needed to trust God for daily sustenance; but I knew better—for I knew just how much money we had and how much food would cost. (God had nothing whatever to do with it.) After ensuring that we ourselves had enough, my next priority was to save so that we could give to various groups who depended on generosity. When I gave, I wanted others to know where the generosity came from. Some of the disciples criticized me in this regard, saying that I was not really being generous; but they were being hypocritical, for they didn't complain when my generosity compelled bystanders and passersby to donate to our cause. (I even thereby proved that the master's teaching was right, for Jesus said, "Give and it will be given to you.")

I was miffed with Mary Magdalene. Rather than selling the expensive perfume that she had, she used it to anoint Jesus. Other disciples were put off because at one time Mary had used the perfume in her seduction of men. I didn't care about what she did, for it had no affect on me. My concerns were more practical: I was annoyed by the fact that Mary could have sold the perfume and deposited the money in the money bag (which was rather light at that time, for in a moment of irresponsibility Jesus gave its contents to poor lepers).

Jesus and I had a falling out over my attitude toward Mary, such that I left the group. (There were other things that led to this falling out, such as Jesus' disregard for the cause of the Zealots.) The argument that I had had with Jesus took place shortly after I had made the arrangements for the last supper, such that I could not fully participate in it. The disciples, who were sweet (but mostly in a sentimental way), *ate the food and drank the wine, and everybody was having a good time, except Jesus—who was talking about the end of the world.*[225] It is just as well that I didn't eat and drink at this meal, for all this talk about the end of the world is nonsense.

Because I had nowhere to turn, I found myself at an inn. Because it reminded me of the stupidity of Jesus, I rejected the wine that the inn-keeper offered me. When I had become tipsy from cheap beer, I told the disheveled inn-keeper about my plight. He must have known one of the priests, for within an hour I found myself talking about the whereabouts of Jesus to a scribe. The scribe wanted information, but he did not seem to know the importance of using discretion. I told him that I would tell him what he wanted to know, but in some place that was more private. We thus went to the facility (I had to piss like a racehorse, anyway). As we entered it, I first checked to make sure that no one was present. The facility was recently occupied, but the patron had left—only a pungent smell lingered. I then told the scribe where Jesus was at that moment. I told him that after I led them to Jesus, I would kiss him. (Like much of what I had done in life, this kiss was altogether backwards, I know; but I reasoned that the kiss would do two things at once: it would identify Jesus, and, more importantly, it would enable me to maintain the honor that others had of me.)

My terms were simple: the officials were not to harm Jesus, and they were to pay me well. (My mind was sober: now that Jesus and his so-called kingdom were out of the picture, I needed money to start a new venture.) While the religious leaders did meet the monetary condition, they failed to keep Jesus from being harmed. When they arrested Jesus, and I saw that great harm was coming to him, I threw the money back to the leaders. I had taken a life wrongfully. Lest my name become synonymous with treachery, I needed to take my own life (doing so would be honorable, I reasoned, for it would protect what others thought of me). After I took my life, I entered into the next world. I there experienced many things that I will now try to recount.

My journey began in a tunnel. At the end of the tunnel was a beautiful light. Were I to assign it a word, I might say that the light was "God"—although I cannot be more specific. Maybe it was Isis, maybe it was Zeus, maybe it was the God of Abraham, or any one of the other countless deities that humanity has worshiped. I don't know.

Accompanying this light were people that I knew but didn't know. What I mean by this is that while I didn't know them, I nevertheless recognized them. No, they were not simply acquaintances, for they were very dear. I assume now that they were people who had encouraged me to embrace and follow goodness; and as I was making my way through the tunnel they were beckoning me.

I then noticed that my senses overlapped: the beckoning had a pleasing aroma, the contours of the tunnel produced soothing music, and the light tasted as sweet as honey.

It was at this point that one part of the tunnel continued toward the light while another veered away. It was not a matter of choosing which direction to go. It's more like I was drawn. As attractive as the light was, there was something within me that resisted it—and the further away that I went from the light, the more I was pleased.

As I journeyed, I did not know when I was asleep or when I was awake, when I was in reality or when I was in a dream (in life I had had the same experience, for I sometimes *awoke from my dreams only to find that I was dead*).[226]

When I at last left the tunnel, I was met by a dog on a shore beside a river. It was not Cerberus, for it was a puppy and not a ferocious beast. It wanted to play tug-of-war or some damned thing. Couldn't it see that I was occupied? I kicked at it, and it whimpered as it slumped off. *I was going somewhere (although I didn't know where),* and the mutt was impeding my progress—so my action was just.[227] (Solomon said that "a righteous man is kind to his animals"—but the puppy was not mine.)

Time and space did not exist. The whole experience was rather collage-like. Even as a single mosaic might depict different scenes at the same time, so my experience included various coterminous episodes.

I noticed the absence of space when I saw other people on the river bank. I loathed the idea of talking to them, even as they had no interest in talking to me. Space concerns the physical relationship between things, and because they were so absorbed in themselves, other selves did not exist—even as I had said in life, *"Islands in the stream, that is what we are."*[228]

I then got on a raft (there was no ferryman, which is a good thing because I had thrown away my coins). As I floated down the river, things got darker. In this darkness I was by myself. I initially thought that *the isolation was perfect*; but, much to my surprise, I couldn't stand not having others around to hear how wonderful I was.[229] I then cried out, *"is there anybody out there?"*[230] There was no response, so I screamed, *"where the hell has everybody gone?"*[231] An answer came from apparitions, who then mournfully sang, "you were to reflect the light." At first I did not understand this; but then I remembered that Jesus had said something similar: he taught that the way that we treat others is a reflection of what we will experience. I then understood what the apparitions were intoning, but, like life itself, this was all backwards. (I also wondered why their singing was dirge-like.) Even my ferry-experience was backwards, for when I got off the ferry I saw the same mutt that I had shooed away—the only difference is that it now cowered with its tail between its legs. I was in a great hurry, but I hadn't moved—this was again akin to my life, in which I could get so ahead of myself that I often forgot where I was going. Indeed, *the more that I toiled to advance, the more backward I went.*[232] No, God did not send me to this *nowhere land.*[233] I sent myself, for one life is but an extension of the other.

Was my experience simply a consequence of oxygen deprivation? No doubt, a case could be made for this. After all, I had tried to hang myself, but because the height was insufficient I ended up asphyxiating myself—or nearly so. Maybe, however, I did die and my experiences were real. (I don't know; existence confuses me.) I have heard about others who have had similar experiences, like Er the soldier. The one thing that convinced me that there was truth to such experiences is that, irrespective of time and place, they share a measure of commonality: crawling through a tunnel to a beautiful light, the confusion of senses, seeing loved ones, and experiencing peace. It would, I think, be foolhardy to be dismissive of the whole matter just because it does not accord with one's worldview. But what does it matter if it was a hallucination or if it was real? Who the hell cares? Reality is as illusory as a dream (both Hesiod and Virgil rightly say that Sleep is the brother of Death).

How I wish that I was not alone, that someone loved me, that someone would say, "*I won't let you choke on the noose around your neck.*"[234] But *no one cares if I should live or die.*[235] Lest others say of me, "*he had no honor in life, and he will have no honor in death,*" I will again try to commit suicide.[236] *Goodbye, sweet people, goodbye. Sweet people, goodbye, goodbye.*[237]

Vignette 38

Unclean Hagar

YEARS AGO MY WOMB had dried up, and I gave birth to a stillborn child. As if God's punishment was not enough, after I gave birth I continued to bleed: I always felt dirty, and the odor was often great.

In keeping with the law of Moses, my husband would not lie with me. The family members all praised him for this righteousness, but they themselves thought ill of me.

My father-in-law, who spent much of the week relaxing, learned of my uncleanness on the Sabbath day. He said to me, "Be sure not to walk too far today, for doing so might make you bleed all the more."

The other daughter-in-law said that in one way she envied my uncleanness because she hated lovemaking. She would say to her husband, "We must abstain one week before and one week after my period, lest we break the law of Moses."

My mother-in-law was also devout. She followed me around with a rag and wiped down everything that I sat on, lest I spread my uncleanness. She often said to me, "Moses said that you are unclean, and sitting on furniture is thus suggestive of your selfishness—for doing so makes others unclean."

I felt like a leper. I was unaccepted by everyone, and I became desperate; so I went on a journey, trying to find healing.

At first I went to various Jewish physicians, but they were not much help. They only told me what I already knew: I must have sinned. I then consulted various Roman physicians, whose prescriptions were too expensive. I then went to an Egyptian specialist; but I said to myself, "I will not forsake my faith, for the law of Moses forbids me to wear an Isis girdle."

I then started to return, but I wanted a longer road because I was hoping to forestall the inevitable, hoping beyond hope that something might happen—whether healing or death. The road that I chose was through an arid valley. It had not rained along that road for months, making even the few plants dry and brittle. Clouds of sand billowed in from the desert, such that my every step wafted dust into the stale air—making everything filthy. *Even though the sun was beginning to set in the East*, it was unbearably hot.[238] At this point, I walked over a bridge that spanned a dying river. I had been wrong in my thinking. I had earlier surmised that this was "the land of the shadow of death" that David had spoken of, but it was more akin to Ezekiel's "valley of dry bones"—for the banks of the river were, even as Aeneas had seen, white with the ossified bones of many people who had judged others. (I was then reminded of the charioteers who drowned on the shores of the Red Sea because they blindly followed the judgment of Pharaoh.) I could not drink the water of the river, because it was more bitter than death—even more bitter than the potion that Moses made faithless women drink (women whose guilt was manifested by bleeding vaginas). I nevertheless sought refuge from the scorching sun in the shade of this bridge; but its refuge was as lifeless as a mirage, for it reminded me of my own desolation. Furthering my despair was my reflection on the river. *I was sad because I thought that at one time it flowed and was teeming with life, but now it was dead.*[239] I also thought that the famed river was aptly named Xyts—for, even as it meandered through lifeless terrain, it had *no exits* from death, and it eventually emptied into the Dead Sea.[240] As I looked more closely at the river, it looked as though it was returning. The Egyptian specialist that I had visited told me about a priestess who, through her incantations, could even stop rivers flowing; but this was even more startling, for the river was was flowing backwards (akin to the shadow that went backwards up the steps of Ahaz). The river, I thought, is just like society—putrid and flowing backwards.

As I sullenly gazed at the dead water, I met a pilgrim on her way to worship in Jerusalem. Like me, she sought refuge under the bridge. I found her to be rather irksome. The way that I was put-off was initially unknown to me, but as I sat with her under the bridge it occurred to me that it was her smile that irritated me—more specifically, the way that her teeth protruded from her mouth whenever she stopped talking. After we exchanged names and expressed empty formalities, feigning piety, I told her that, like David, she longed for God "in a dry and weary land where there is no water" (my real concern was to prompt her to give me some water from her water skin).

She said in reply that when David thirsted for the waters of Bethlehem, God provided a messenger to get such water. While she did not have much water herself, she then gave me water to slake my thirst (rather selfishly, I admit, I used some of the water to wipe my brow). Upon seeing that my body was replenished, and overlooking my apparent selfishness, she then jabbered about this and that (which I welcomed, as talking kept her from smiling and me seeing her ugly mouth). Among other things, she pointed out a desert flower that had bloomed in magnificence. She noted that, far from wilting, it thrived in the arid climate. As if she was reading my thoughts about the river, she then said that Virgil was wrong in referring to this river as the river of no return, as if there is no hope for those who are wrongly despised. While, she went on, God tells his people through Moses, "Return to dust, O sons of men," people rest in the knowledge that God, who "rules over Rahab, Leviathan, and the hostile rivers," has depthless mercy. She went on to say that the same God who said through Moses, "Do not return to godless Egypt" is the one who, in his mercy, made the Jordan cease flowing so that people could live in the land of promise. I nodded in agreement, but this was only a polite thing to do; my real concern had been met.

After my weary body I had rested, my way resumed I on the desert slope.[241] I stood up to go—sitting with the pilgrim under that accursed bridge was worse than trudging under the relentless sun. After I crossed the bridge, I nevertheless reprimanded myself for not wishing the pilgrim the best; but as I turned to do so, she was nowhere to be seen. I then thought that, like the desert experience of my namesake, perhaps she had been a messenger from God. I then judged myself for treating her in such an ill fashion. Worse, I thought, than being selfish and feigning piety, was thinking less of her because she had buckteeth. So also, I wrongly assumed that because she was so ugly she could not be an instrument of God to help me on my way. God, I had previously thought, was most present in things that are glorious and impressive.

I slowed my pace when I saw that the single road became *two roads that diverged in the Wild Wood*: the one was smooth and broad while the other was treacherous and narrow.[242] A rider on a pale horse then appeared on the broad way. I asked its withered rider, whose name was *Everyman*, which way I should go, but he could not answer me.[243] He seemed to have great knowledge about himself, but he did not know where he came from or where he was going to—even though he seemed to be in a hurry. Partly because of my disenchantment with him, I chose the narrow way. (I should like to think, however, that my faith had *made all the difference*, for

Solomon said that "there is a way that seems right to people but it leads to death"—even as Moses similarly taught about the two paths.)[244] While on the narrow way, I ascended to a *temperate* plateau *smelling of vegetation* and noticed a commotion in the distance.[245] I quickened my pace and saw a crowd following a man named Jesus. My heart pounded for I had heard that Jesus was a healer, and that divine power emanated from him. I said to myself, "If I can just get close enough to him, maybe some of his power will transfer to me." I approached him from behind, and then touched his stained garment. Sensing that power had gone out from him, Jesus turned around and asked, "Who touched me?" Others were angry with me because Jesus was on his way to help a sick girl, and I had interrupted him. I sheepishly confessed that it was I who had touched him. Far from being angry or thinking that he had been interrupted, its as if time was no more and that I was the only one who existed. Jesus then looked at me directly and said, "Your faith has cleansed you." I left the crowd and washed myself to see if the bleeding would continue. It had stopped. Prior to worshiping the God of Moses, I then cleansed myself in a mikveh.

Because of my journey, I have learned that being clean involves seeing beauty within the madness of society. Was I myself mad when I saw the sun set in the East? Did the river flow backwards? Was the pilgrim an angel? Such counter-intuitive experiences could be explained in different ways. Perhaps my vision had been impaired from the sun; or, perhaps, I was deluded because I was exhausted. I was, after all, tired of life, and it seemed to me that human society is topsy-turvy: "Why," I asked myself, "do we judge others for things that they cannot control?" Perhaps, however, my despair caused me to see through the insanity of society.

As I look back on the experience, I often ask the question, "why did all of this happen?" I am not sure why, and I may never know. Perhaps people are used by God both for evil and for good. Why shouldn't it be this way? God works through people to achieve his will: God made the serpent who deceived Eve, only to bless humanity; he hardened Pharaoh so that my people could cross the Sea; and he used the evil Assyrians and Babylonians to punish Israel, only to promise a greater crossing. Perhaps I can understand my own sufferings in this way: it was wrong for family members to reject me as they did, but God used their ugly legalism to create beauty within me. When I am trying to understand my story, it is also helpful to think of the story of Jesus. When he was on that de-branched tree, he knew that it was people who did this, not God. All the same, perhaps some good will come out of his death.

Vignette 39

Believing Thomas

I ASKED JESUS WHAT truth is. He said, "I am the way, the truth, and the life." His answer mystified me. "How," I asked myself, "can a person be the truth?" Perhaps, I thought, Jesus misunderstood me. I wanted the facts.

When the disciples told me that Jesus had risen from the dead, I initially got angry at them—but I calmed down when I realized that their claim was consistent with their crass emotionalism. They had been on an emotional high when, just one week earlier, throngs of people had hailed Jesus as the messiah; but their hopes of a messianic kingdom were laid asunder when the limp body of Jesus was placed in a tomb. The disciples returned to their high when they were told that Jesus had risen.

I did not believe that Jesus had risen; I needed to be convinced before I would believe. To my great surprise, I became convinced: the disciples and I were together, and while they excitedly talked about the resurrection of Jesus, I was sullen and depressed. At this moment, Jesus himself appeared (I don't know how, for the doors were locked). While he invited me to touch his hands to know that it was really him, I didn't need any convincing.

I then devoted the better part of a decade to defending the plausibility of belief in the resurrection. I did so in many ways. I first noted that various scriptures spoke of how the messiah would rise from the dead. The authors wrote of how the messiah would be beaten, how he would be crucified, how his garments would be gambled for, how he would thirst, where he would be buried, how he would live again—and, most astoundingly, how nations would put their trust in him. I also noted how various stories anticipated the story of Jesus. In the Exodus story, for example, we read that only those whose doors are covered by the blood of an unblemished lamb would be delivered from Egypt, and in the Jesus story we know that only those who are covered by the blood of the innocent Lamb will be delivered and enter the land of promise. What the ancient prophets wrote amazed me. I also noted that the first witnesses to the resurrection were women. Because this was embarrassing to early believers (for society does not recognize the testimony of women), they changed the story to make men the first witnesses. Far from undermining the story, the fact that it was changed is suggestive of its early existence: they changed only what they thought was embarrassing. I similarly noted that one witness to the resurrection was James, the brother of Jesus. During the time that Jesus was preaching, James thought that his brother was crazy. But after the crucifixion of Jesus, James changed dramatically: while he himself was initially hostile to the message of his brother, James had since become a believer—even becoming a martyr because he believed in the resurrection. How can one explain such change? It is again suggestive that the resurrection did indeed happen.

"Suggestive that" but not "proof that." Neither the scriptures, nor eyewitness testimony, nor how stories underwent change provide "proof" of the resurrection. One can, at best, say that belief is more plausible than unbelief.

When Jesus invited me to touch his wounds I did not need to touch him; the invitation was enough—even as seeking Jewels will say, "*I felt the touch of God.*"[246] I did not need to touch him; the invitation was enough. The whole experience captivated me, such that I confessed "my Lord and my God." It was my confession that is the stuff of faith. (Even as I did not need to touch him, I pray that he himself will always *touch me and take me to that other place.*)[247]

My experience of Jesus at that moment is in accord with how miracles are experienced. For those with eyes to see, everything in existence is imbued with the miraculous: from the heavens to the little child—and everything above, below, and in between. To people without eyes, however, even *if one were to produce a wonder, such people would do their utmost to explain away the wonder rather than confessing that it exists* (for people believe what makes them happy, not as they say, with proof).[248] I simply don't understand why people say that they will only believe something if it can first be proven: personal tastes cannot be proven, but such things are cherished; the world of goodness is undeniable, but such a world cannot be proven; and people's love for others is certain, but such love is, similarly, beyond proof. (It is inconsistent for a Cynic to insist that faith be proven but not at the same time demand that proof be proven: faith and proof are equally based on sets of assumptions that can neither be affirmed nor denied. They can only be accepted as givens—which is a central ingredient of faith.)

I did not only concern myself with the resurrection. I also thought about the claims that he made to be one with God. No doubt, as they recounted what Jesus did, the disciples often put words in his mouth. Jesus did not, to be sure, ever say that he is God. But he did not have to say as much, for his actions spoke as loudly as any of his words. Upon healing a cripple, for instance, he said "The Son of Man forgives sins." So also, upon being chastised for breaking the Sabbath Day, Jesus told people that he is "Lord of the Sabbath." Again, after the sea ceased from its raging when Jesus rebuked it, his disciples queried, "Who is this that even calms the wind and the waves?" The point is not if he actually calmed the storm; the point is that his disciples believed that he did so. The words of Jesus were one with his actions, and we must look at his actions as much as we listen to his words to understand what he thought about himself.

A meeting was convened in Jerusalem to discuss the resurrection. All the disciples agreed that the good news should be brought to every nation. Because I had had experience with lands to the distant east, I happily consented to being a missionary; but because I was one of the original twelve, people thought that it was important for me to stay in Judea for a time.

(One thing that I did while still in Judea was assemble a collection of the sayings of Jesus. Doing so was easy because I had heard Jesus preach and teach scores of times. No doubt, my collection may well be updated— sayings may be added, or believers might unite such sayings with the story of Jesus. It really doesn't matter, for I have confidence that the collection will further the truth of Jesus.)

When, at long last, I voyaged to the eastern lands, I was confronted with how to present the truth of Jesus. Doing so was not so simple as one might think, for the people in eastern lands have little in common with Jews. Indeed, most of them knew nothing about the Hebrew scriptures. How, then, was I to communicate that Jesus was the long-awaited messiah?

Consistent with the fact that all truth is God's truth, I found that various teachings within the faith of eastern people complemented the good news. This is especially true of the subject of desire. While Jesus had much to say about the necessity of dying to oneself, he said little about the mechanics involved in doing just that: how, practically, does one die to oneself?

What must one do? My friends from the east have emphasized that one can extinguish desire through meditation.

This is not at all to say that one must never challenge elements within their faith, for I found that various aspects of their faith were antithetical to faith in Jesus. Let us think, yet again, of desire. I concur with Buddha: "everything is burning with desire." (Indeed, two things have led to faithlessness in my life include getting what I want and not getting what I want: *I can't always get what I want*, and even when I get it, *I can't get no satisfaction!*)[249] But desire, in itself, is not the problem, for God loves us as he made us—and he made us with desire. The problem is that we desire the wrong things: we desire ourselves rather than the One who disguises himself in others. Desiring self at the expense of others is the contagion from which we need to be healed, and such healing comes in spades when we see ourselves in others.

The subject of karma is another example of how ideas can be antithetical to the gospel. Karma teaches that one gets what one deserves: either in this life or in a life to come, goodness will come to one who lives an upright life, and judgment will come to those who do not live as they ought to. Central to the faith of Jesus are the subjects of mercy and non-condemnation—subjects that are entirely contrary to karma. Where karma teaches that one gets what one deserves, grace teaches the opposite—one receives mercy simply because it is in the very nature of God to be generous, both to the righteous and the wicked alike. *Grace travels outside of karma and makes beauty out of ugly things*—such that living in love is the effect, not the cause, of mercy.[250]

After I had started communities of faith in that eastern land, I returned to Judea. While the leaders in Jerusalem were excited about what I reported, some of them still referred to me as a doubter. This hurt me, and I felt sorry for such people, for they failed to see that there can be great faith in doubt. It is actually the one who is afraid of doubt who has little faith, for *there is more faith in honest doubts than in any creed*.[251] Maybe they have never experienced the fact that God is greater than their beliefs about him. I myself experienced this overwhelmingly, for just when I thought that I was abandoning God because I did not believe, that is precisely when God found me—*his beauty trumped my doubt*.[252] (I often laugh with tears as I ask God, "Why have you been so good to me?") As I look back on my journey, I see that God used my doubts to create greater faith in me. It is, for instance, because of my doubts that I understand the patience of God.

I have learned that God is not holding a big stick to smite me with just as soon as I think the wrong way about something. God himself guided me through my season of doubt because he knew that I would not be *honest to God* if I did not go through it.[253] It is also because of my doubts that I have more empathy toward those who are finding their way. Rather than being suspicious of falsehood, or correcting erring people whenever they advance a thought that is contrary to what I think is truth, I smile and say to myself, "God will lead them." All the same, I do want to invite people to reflect on their lives—especially so when I see humble doubt morphing into angry cynicism.

Like me, Pilate asked Jesus, "What is truth?" Perhaps because he knew that Pilate was not yet ready to hear, Jesus did not answer. Truth, I remind myself, is not simply the facts, but the life of God that is experienced through Jesus.

Vignette 40

Cassandra, the Caustic Prophetess

CASSANDRA WAS BORN CLOSE to the end of the reign of Caligula and she died during Trajan's reign. Having lived while many emperors ruled, and because she was married to a general, Cassandra had a good understanding of the Empire. Cassandra converted from devotion to Dionysus to worship of Jesus when she was still young, not long after her first husband had been murdered.

While at sea, brigands from another ship overtook the ship that she was on, killed the men (including her husband), and placed Cassandra and a female slave, named Boethia, in a boat. They said, "If the gods so will it, you will be rescued." Some of the brigands were, ironically, from devout homes. Owing in part to their godly upbringings, even as they maliciously made the boat rudderless, they mercifully provided Cassandra and Boethia with provisions. Shortly after they were set adrift, Boethia prayed, "help, Lord, for the sea is so big and my boat is so small." She was then calm, reminding herself that she was in the hands of God. Boethia's tranquility came from the marriage of Stoicism and faith in Jesus: Stoicism had taught her that circumstances are fleeting; and faith in Jesus had given her hope—for while Jesus had also been a slave ravaged by cruelty, he was victorious. Even as their food and water were almost depleted, and even as the wind and waves buffeted the small boat, Boethia was quiet. Cassandra envied this calm, such that she wanted it for herself. (Beauty itself created such desire through the dire circumstance—Beauty that had whispered, "trust me.")

Not long into the drifting, Cassandra's hopes for deliverance were dashed when, upon coming close to the shoreline, she saw the waves pummeling a cliff. Making matters yet worse, the boat seemed to be drifting into a whirlpool. Cassandra fretted that this whirlpool was none other than that of Odysseus's Charbydis, and that Scylla the monster would soon appear to devour them. Even as she frantically sought to paddle the boat with her hands, she yelled at Boethia for help. Boethia, *who had fallen asleep at the stern*, awoke to the screams of Cassandra; but, *standing up, she rebuked* Cassandra: *"Quiet, be still; please, please, please, get up off your knees, for frantically praying won't do you no good.*[254] What you need is a calm faith. If, indeed, we are in the whirlpool of Charbydis, fretting and being full of fear will only make things worse. The turbulence of the waters is similarly proportionate to trust: *the greater the trust, the calmer the waters will appear to be*—better than flailing at the surface is to be at rest, like the waters that lie at the depths of the sea. Even as the wind and the waves buffet the boat, lie down in in it so that you do not exaggerate the circumstance. Look only to the heavens and say, 'I trust you.'"[255] As it turned out, they were not in a whirlpool—the fears of Cassandra were only in her mind. Cassandra then asked herself, "What god has possessed Boethia such that she is so calm in the midst of angry waves?" As if led by Providence, they then drifted toward an island inhabited by pagans (one might even call them *anonymous believers*, for they were certainly more righteous than the brigands).[256] It was a this point that Cassandra converted to Jesus ("Beauty," she said, *"whispered to me when the waters were calm, but shouted to me when the waves billowed.")*[257]

Years later, the Christian faith of Cassandra was a problem to her second husband, who was a general, for anything Jewish was treasonous (early Christians referred to Jesus, not to the emperor, as the King of kings). Cassandra nevertheless promised her husband to keep things quiet.

Cassandra said that even while Jesus was alive many of his sayings were collected. These collections of sayings were then brought together, and some were mixed with the story of Jesus—particularly his trial, death, and resurrection. While this process was taking place, missionaries spread both the teachings of Jesus and the ramifications of his crucifixion and resurrection.

Concerning the crucifixion and resurrection, Cassandra said, "I was always a little suspicious of the letters of Paul. I was baptized into the faith of Jesus, not into the faith of Jesus as interpreted by Paul. Yes, Jesus died for sinners and rose again; but I don't need Paul's letters to teach me this. As much as Paul's letters use language that is suggestive of living faith, moreover, implicit to them is that faith is only real if it conforms to a particular understanding of the crucifixion and resurrection. What Paul was advancing was a system, a paradigm that says, 'you must believe such and such and you must not believe such and such.' Why, indeed, have we placed such confidence in Paul's letters? Their testimony is only as good as is Paul's contention that truth was revealed to him. Why are we putting such trust in one man who heard voices? All the same, maybe I am not being fair to Paul. He did not, after all, think that he was writing scripture; he was only writing letters."

"Not unlike the authority accorded to the letters of Paul, I am put-off by a creed that is in the works. The would-be creed goes from 'I believe that Jesus was born of a virgin' directly to 'I believe that Jesus was crucified under Pontius Pilate.' Not a whisper is given to that fact that the Son of Man might have had something worthwhile to say! What a sacred undoing of all that is holy, a godless omission that only the serpent could devise! (Did not the voice from heaven say, 'Here is my Son. Listen to him'?) I understand the motivation behind the creed. One concern is to keep gnostic thinking out of the faith. Jesus was not a disembodied spirit, as gnostics suppose; but worse than gnosticism is the buffoonery of trying to protect the truth of Jesus by overlooking his teachings. Indeed, the framers of the creed have themselves become gnostic, for by omitting the teaching of Jesus they are unwittingly making Christian faith a matter of mind—reducing it to thinking the right way about things."

Cassandra then discussed the divide between the Jesus sect and the rest of Judaism.

"Because the Jesus sect was becoming powerful, it was inevitable that it would separate from the faith of the fathers. This divide was furthered by the destruction of the temple: whereas some said that God destroyed the temple because of the Christian sin, others said that God did so because of the Jewish sin. The division grew, and many leaders did whatever they could to drive a wedge between the two groups. At the end of the synagogue service, for instance, an invocation has been introduced that makes Christians enemies of the faith. Both groups have similarly used scriptures against each other. Judaism has said, 'these books, and no others, define our faith,' even as Christianity has said, 'Jewish scripture and various texts about Jesus define our faith.' Christianity was no longer a sect of Judaism, but, like Judaism, it had become a religion."

Largely because Cassandra had once been a devotee of Dionysus (in which untamed emotions could be expressed ecstatically), upon becoming a Christian she naturally became a prophetess. Her prophesying was informed—both because she had a firm grasp of the history of the Empire, and because she understood Christian faith. Sadly, however, as correct as they might have been, her prophecies were not believed.

While at a church that met in a catacomb under the streets of Rome, as if she was in a trance, Cassandra prophesied: "Only slaves and children have an innate awareness of what it means to follow Jesus. Everyone else is blinded by power. Because of lust for power, I predict that Christianity will transmogrify into Christendom. At present, we see that the Empire is using religion to defend itself—'a true citizen of the Empire devoutly worships the emperor.' Christendom will similarly use the Empire to defend itself—'forsaking the Empire is to forsake Christ, for the Empire is Christ's.' To maintain power, both groups will have at their disposal arrows, spears, and swords. They will only differ in how they use such weapons: the Empire will use the sword to expand its frontiers; and Christendom *will make the sword into a sacrament* (killing someone who does not believe in the mercy of Jesus).[258] Here we see *idolatrous ideologies* at their worst.[259] All the same, it is easier to overlook Rome's lust for power than Christendom's lust, for while politics is unapologetic about power, Jesus taught that divine power comes through weakness."

Cassandra then ceased speaking in Latin, only to speak in a heavenly tongue. An interpreter retold what she was saying.

"One child of power is orthodoxy. It is not, Christendom will assert, how one lives but how one thinks that is most important. If people do not think the right way, they will be branded as heretics and unbelievers worthy of death. But his is all backwards, for *the lives of people are bigger than any big idea.*[260] On that great day, God will not ask, 'What did you think?' but 'How did you live?' It is similarly from such a demonic understanding of power that leaders will insist that right definitions are used. No doubt, they will say that one needs to define in order to understand; but the real concern is knowing about, not knowing. The stupidity of Christendom will be so great that it will assert (even as it is religiously stoned) that religion is *an opiate for the masses,*[261] and that *God is dead* (only as a crucified one could say).[262] The hypocrisy in such disavowals is that while Christendom will try to rid itself of God, it will do so in a Christian way—but it will not rid the world of conscience. It will not, because it cannot. That we are our brother's keeper can never be erased from the heart, for the great commandment to love is intractable—even though Christendom *will say it wants the kingdom but doesn't want God in it*, the kingdom of God will nevertheless shine through its hypocrisy.[263] Yes, the tree will become gigantic, even covering the earth, but it will use refuse to grow."

Vignette 41

Augustyne, the Thinker

I REMEMBER AS A boy looking up at the night sky and wondering. Because I often plagued my mother with questions, I asked her what was past the stars. "Other stars," she glibly answered. I then asked her what was beyond those stars. Thinking that I was again being insolent, my mother said, "beyond those stars is a place of torment for boys who ask too many questions." My mother then reprimanded me: "*If you want to kiss the sky, you'd better learn how to kneel. On your knees, boy!*"[264] Mom was right; I now study upon my knees, for I know that *the way of prayer is the way of belief.*[265]

I have always had questions, but not for reasons of pride. I have known that the ocean of eternity could never exist in my tiny mind. My motivation for querying is a reflection of my yearning to know and love God.

As I trek to the summit of truth, I happily recognize that my every step is grounded in humble belief—and the more that I know this, the less arduous the hike is, for truth is humble. (Truth is powerful in its humility: it is like water in this regard—for even as water strives for the lowest place, it slowly carves away the hardest stone.) Philosophers often assume that reason can bring one to truth. The problem with this assumption is that because reason is often accompanied by pride, it cannot ascend to the summit of truth.

In my earlier years, I tried to find truth only through reason. This changed when I heard children playing on the other side of a courtyard wall. The children were saying, "*pick up and read; pick up and read.*"[266] While this was part of their game, I nevertheless regarded it as the voice of the Spirit—for at that very time I saw a scripture scroll on a table. Without delay, I picked up the scroll and there read about righteousness. It was, similarly, a child who helped me to understand the relationship between reason and faith. While walking on the beach one day, I puzzled over how Christ could be completely human and completely divine at the same time. No rational explanation seemed to do justice to this truth. I then saw a boy in the distance who was digging a hole in the sand, running to the sea, filling his pail with water, and then hastening back to dump the water into the hole. I asked the boy what he was doing. "I am putting the sea into the hole," the boy said. I smirked and said, "What you are trying to do is impossible." "Your attempt," he said, "to put eternity into your tiny mind is similarly impossible." Reason, I then reminded myself, can only point to truth; it cannot fully explain truth.

Reason does not like to bend its knee before anything else. As to the most basic of all questions, for example, as to why something rather than nothing exists, reason has nothing to say. Reason is arrogantly silent at this point because it knows that it is only reasonable when it acknowledges that it is itself based on awareness.

I have similarly thought that we think about time in a most unreasonable way. We all know what time is, but when we try to reason it we have troubles—for time can only be experienced, it cannot be reasoned. With regard to the present, I happily note that, at the philosophical level, *tomorrow never happens*, for at the very moment that I think about the present, it becomes the past, and insofar as I anticipate its presence, the present becomes part of the future.[267] But thanks be to God that "the philosophical level" is not synonymous with "the real level"—for while we cannot define the present, we are aware that it exists.

With regard to the past, the Christian is concerned with it insofar as doing so assists the present: we remember the love of God in the past in order that we might live such love in the present.

Such re-invoking of the past to strengthen the present should occur every day. I recall being depressed years ago. Late one evening, I paddled a boat in a lake. With the exception of the occasional jumping fish, the water was still. A full moon shimmered on the surface of the lake and gently lit the calm. I set my paddle down in the canoe and said to myself, "remember this." When I am stressed, I remember that my soul can be as serene as that lake. I have also surmised that just as the lake's reflection of the heavens is proportionate to the lake's stillness, so the reflection of God in my life comes from calm.

(A distant relation of Jesus similarly likened the wise person to a man who, while fleeing from a lion, falls over a cliff but grasps a root—only to see that if he survived the fall, another lion at the base of the cliff would devour him. The man then sees a mouse nibbling at the root. At this moment his demise seems to be as certain as it is imminent; but then the man sees a tasty berry within his grasp, and all his fears vanish: he has ceased fixating on his ordeal to think about the scrumptious berry—all that matters is enjoying the moment and not fearing what the future may or may not hold.)

With regard to the future, like the past, it becomes prominent for the Christian when its concern is love in the present. The marriage of the present to the future creates hope. The important thing is to live in the present as if one was living in the future, and this is hope. Jesus calls us to live in such hope, the eternal now, for eternity is embraced whenever one lives in hope—such that *we can take eternity just a minute at a time*.[268]

The Lord's prayer says as much: "Your kingdom come, your will be done, on earth as it is in heaven." What is seen in the Lord's prayer is equally present in various stories. When the first couple ate of the forbidden fruit (or when Pandora tipped over her jar), evils that ail humanity came like a flood, for the couple chose themselves rather than God. In his grace, though, God told people that if they live in hope (the one thing that did not leave Pandora's jar), eternity could be tasted in the now. I say "tasted" carefully: while it is true that "no mind has conceived what God has promised for those who love him," there will nevertheless be a certain "been there, done that" in the hereafter. While we will be swept away with love and mercy, none of this will take us unawares as if we had never tasted such things before. The believer says, "*I gotta taste of paradise, and I'm never gonna let it slip away.*"[269]

For the believer, then, future hope shapes present life. Insofar as we can hear in the present a whisper of eternity, the present is transfigured. The one whose present is colored by the future sees the beauty of eternity in all things: the stone of Mount Sinai becomes the moss of the Mount of Beatitudes; a sanatorium becomes a spa; and a prison house becomes a house of freedom. Whatever we read, hear, or see, we interpret through eternity— for all things in the here and now point to the there and the then: love in this life points to a greater love; patience toward someone is a whisper of divine long-suffering; and the joys that we taste in this life are anticipations of eternal felicity. To those with eyes that can see, even unsavory attitudes remind one of goodness: judgmentalism whispers that we are accepted; lust is a broken reciprocal of Love; and violence is done away with by mercy.

Consistent with the timeless nature of eternity, people in the present are influenced by what people in the future will say. It's as if a musician, a bard, a poet, or a novelist taps into the world of the future, such that future thoughts shape present reality. (Can I prove this? No more than I can prove that something outside myself exists. As with the best of human thought, I am speculating carefully.) Two analogies from nature may be used: a tree is in its present seed, and the present caterpillar will become the future butterfly.

Please don't judge me for being heady. My discussion may be cloaked in abstractions, but do know that my concerns are practical. Even as I am writing this, I am gazing at the sundial. I am fretting and saying to myself, "Do you have time to write, or should you get ready for your visitors?" (But the eternal now says, "your writing is preparing for your visitors.") When the visitors come, I will not want them to stay longer than what is socially acceptable. (But if they should do so, the eternal now may say, "perhaps they have concerns that they cannot express.") The eternal now tells me to breathe in life for every breath might be my last, that every moment is my life. No, *time doesn't wait for me, for it keeps on flowing with the grace from the Lord above.*[270] (Pythagoras, that insightful pagan, was right when he said that "time itself glides on with constant motion, ever as a flowing river.") I must, therefore, become part of this life-giving current.

I want to be practical by saying more about hope.

Some years ago, I visited a prisoner who was chained to a wall. He enthusiastically showed me designs he could make with his chains. Because the stench was so bad, I could only marvel at his designs through misty eyes.

The prisoner then asked me with the same enthusiasm that he had with making designs, "Do you think that the end of the world is fast approaching?" I said to him, "If your guard kills you tonight, your end has come; what difference does it make if the world ends today or tomorrow?" The prisoner did not understand me. I do empathize with him, for knowing when the final battle would take place gave him some measure of hope. Seeing that I would not answer his question about the end of the world the way he wanted, the prisoner then asked me, "What would you do if you knew that today was your last day?" Adding salt to the wound, I said, "*I would plant an apple tree.*"[271] What I meant by this is that my last day must be like any other day. Because what I said again escaped his understanding, he started to fidget. The prisoner then said, "*I got, got, got, got no time* for prattling about abstractions."[272]

The prisoner then told me that, upon being released, he could get a job working in his father's vineyard. He said that he had misgivings, however, for he did not like his father—in part, because of how his father had failed to protect him; and in part, because he was jealous of his "elder brother" who was at one time chained to the same wall, but who had since been working in his father's vineyard. "What," the prisoner asked, "should I do when I get out of prison?" I answered, "love God and do what you want." The prisoner was visibly perturbed, for he thought that such thinking sanctions lawlessness—the very thing that got him into prison. But I explained myself. By saying "love God and do what you want," I was endorsing neither antinomian nor libertine thought. I explained to him that if we love God we will do what he wants, for our natures will change. The prisoner thought, yet again, that I was avoiding a straightforward answer; and our meeting abruptly ended when the prisoner said that he wanted to relieve himself in his pot.

Time had a vital role to play both in the prisoner and in me. Regarding the prisoner, he was chained to careless thinking. As for me, because I did not have enough sleep, and because I was unnecessarily stressed, I was short with him. I have learned that one of the most important things that I need to do to walk in the love of God is, quite simply, to be mindful of my own neediness! Adam's transgression (*which is also my sin, though it were done before*) gets the best of me when I have not had enough sleep.[273]

Back, then, to "abstractions" . . .

We must ask ourselves about the origin of time. Time had a beginning, for, as Aristotle implied, if an infinite number of events took place before today, then today would never have arrived.

The philosophers are correct in asserting that the Logos created time. The Logos existed before time, then created time, and now works in time—even as the Logos itself exists outside of time. (This belief is universal, for Thomas, who is familiar with eastern thought, says that the "Tao" is similar to the "Logos.") While Christian faith agrees with what the philosophers have said about the Logos, it nevertheless differs in that it knows the Logos not as an impersonal force (an "it"), but as a personal force (a "he"). The Logos became human in Jesus, such that when we follow his teachings we are in sync with the cosmos.

Again, I want to be practical. The teaching that the Logos became flesh has tremendous implications for how Christians live. A poetic sentence that summarizes this teaching is the following: "The Son of God became the Son of Man so that sons of men might become sons of God." The "so that" of this sentence captures why the Logos became flesh—"so that" people might become who they are supposed to be.

I was recently asked by an unbeliever what God was doing before he created time. I responded with the thoughts of my mother: "*God was making hell for those who are governed by silly questions.*"[274]

Vignette 42

Heraclus, the Christian

YESTERDAY MY GRANDSON TOLD me that I am too skinny. He remarked that he could see how my tendons and ligaments work together to move my limbs. He noted the same thing about my neck, which he likened to a sapling that twists. He similarly said that he could see how my sinews and muscles work in unison to produce expressions—whether it was laughter, or, as at this time, growing impatience! I told my grandson to stop his incessant chatter. He nevertheless persisted as he gazed at my legs; but he ceased when his mother called him for dinner—like all humanity, his physical appetite proved to be more important than his opinions.

What my grandson said of me is equally true of all nature: everything is connected. Take an eddy, for example. Often behind a protruding boulder, one notes that the water, which only a moment earlier was swiftly moving, suddenly slows down. This quiet water then gently swirls around a vortex—in which the waters that are at a greater distance from the vortex move slowly while the waters that are at a smaller distance move more rapidly. The vortex itself twists in a dance-like motion. If it could talk, one droplet in the vortex might say to another, "I have met you before" or "I collided with you in the rapids and now I am different." Each droplet is unique, but as each droplet interacts with other droplets, its uniqueness changes. When we have such an awareness, we say with Archimedes, "Eureka! Eureka!" We then realize that *what all that humanity is looking for is found in a little water.*[275]

My grandson and I were recently exploring life within a small tidal pool. At one point we saw a crab approaching the pool. My grandson wondered if the minnows in the pool were worried that the crab might invade their space. (While I may not be mentally challenged like him, I, too, was worried.) A wave then came, the pool disappeared, and the minnows and crab were dispersed. The wave, which soaked us, washed away our worries and made our questions moot. The change that the wave brought was good; but I don't typically like change. So long as things are working, I want things to stay the same. But this is never the case, for the only thing that is unchangeable is change—such that wisdom teaches that one's focus should not be on what ought to be but on what is.

(The thinking that everything is changing and interconnected is also true of the mental universe. Whether it is the dreams that people have, their common convictions, or the myths, legends and meta-narratives that they share, there seems to be a universal stream of consciousness, a web in which interconnected minds *whisper eternity*: Odysseus may have captained the ship that Jonah boarded; and while Jonah and Aeneas shared a berth, they were both reprimanded for not caring about others—Mercury chastised the son of the goddess, and the sailors scolded the prophet of God.)[276]

Not unlike my grandson, my friend Augustyne has enriched my life.

While Augustyne is fascinated by time and I am interested in space, our common interests merge in the Christ event. Christ is the center of both time and space: things before Christ anticipated him, things after him look back to him; and the cross is the nexus of heaven and earth.

There are also differences between myself and Augustyne.

Augustyne likes to recount how the Spirit has worked in him. He says that as children were playing a game, they said, "pick up and read; pick up and read." Believing that this was the voice of the Spirit, Augustyne then picked up a scripture scroll and read about righteousness. Augustyne also fondly recounts how a child on a beach helped him to understand the relationship between faith and reason. Augustyne has since done an amazing job in synthesizing the God-given scriptures with real life. While I rejoice in how God has used Augustyne, I do have problems with his synthesis, which often seems to be more based more on reason than experience. It's not that I disagree with him on any one point, it's just that I am not so positive. His ideas are too precise, too refined; and they don't do justice to material existence, or, more specifically, human frailty. In my mind, Augustyne would have a better understanding of God if he had played with the children on the street and made sandcastles with the boy on the beach, for God "has hidden truth from the wise and learned and revealed it to little children."

While we were at the gymnasium together, I remember talking to Augustyne about how the heart shapes reason. I said to him that *the heart has reasons of which reason knows nothing.*[277] I also said that truth is known not only as it is thought about, but also as it is experienced.

(Two other members at the gymnasium overheard our conversation. The leader of the two had great self-confidence, while the other seemed to be an empty shell, *a complete unknown who pretended to be someone that he was not.*[278] The leader agreed with Augustyne that reason eclipses all other faculties; but the other, who was akin to cursed Echo, did not have his own thoughts, for he could only repeat what this Narcissus said.)

Augustyne had little, if any, regard for what I had said. What I thought was arrogance angered me—such that I was tempted to let the weight that he was using fall upon him! While I did avoid falling prey to the temptation, I said the following to him, "What is true of the heart is equally true of life experiences. *When I wake up beside my wife whom I love,*[279] feelings of awe overcome me, feelings that cannot be expressed by words, and such feelings lead me to ponder upon the kindness of God, for I then joyously query, 'What did I do to deserve such a precious wife?'[280] 'How,' I repeatedly ask myself, 'could beauty be so kind to an ordinary guy?'[281] I ask such questions even as I delight in my wife's morning breath: while it wreaks to the third heaven, it is as fragrant as a rose—for in it she says, 'I adore you.' I don't know my wife because I can tell you how many bones she has, because I can count how many hairs are on her head, or because I know how tall she is. I know my wife because I empathize with what she feels."

Augustyne looked unimpressed, but I nevertheless continued, "As you know, there is something about relationships that cannot be neatly explained, something visceral. Whatever the relationship might be, be it romantic or filial, Platonic or collegial—every relationship has a quality that cannot be described, only felt. So also, how might one explain the fragrance of a rose to someone who does not have the sense of smell? *All language would be insufficient.*[282] The closest that words will ever come when trying to describe the fragrance of the rose will be poetic: superb comparisons and metaphors may abound, but the fragrance of the rose can only be known as it is experienced. What is true of the rose is equally true of music, the bouquet of wine, the taste of food, and the worlds of ethics and beauty. Our knowledge of things transcends our ability to describe them. At the very best, carefully chosen words only point to such things. This equally holds for truth, for what *we can't explain we can nevertheless feel somehow.*"[283]

Augustyne replied, "It matters not where I am or what I've experienced. All that I need is quiet humility, and I can employ reason to arrive at truth."

Because I was exasperated, I blurted out, "*Don't analyze, don't analyze, don't go that way, don't live that way, that would paralyze your evolution.*[284] I then calmed myself (I had to do so to communicate with my rational friend) by saying, "Truth is not something that you 'arrive at' but something that finds you even as you journey in and toward it. Truth is not something that you know about, as if it were outside of you, but it is something within you. Truth, moreover, must not be limited to ideas, for ideas can at best provide a foundation upon which truth manifests itself. Your 'all that I need' similarly suggests that human reasoning is reliant on human comfort—one cannot reason if one is tired, if one is hungry, or if one's bowels have not been emptied." Rather facetiously, I then said, "but don't let your humanity obscure your ability to reason."

In much of his writings, Augustyne rightly deprecates pride and stresses the importance of humility. It seems to me, however, that for Augustyne humility is just another idea that is to be thought about. It is not an awareness that is to be experienced. (There is even hidden pride in his flourishes against pride, for he uses clever rhetorical devices to castigate rhetoric!) Up until now, *Augustyne has, similarly, tried to explain the kingdom of this world, but the point is to change it* so that it mirrors the kingdom of heaven—a kingdom that is experienced even as it is talked about.[285] *What, after all, does it profit a man to discourse profoundly on who God is, but be devoid of humility, and thereby displease God?*[286] Defining humility in the right way is infinitely far from actually being humble. Doing so is as darkly futile as those in Tartarus who eternally try to fill a basin with water in pails but are unable to do so because the pails have holes in them.

I doubt very much if, on this side of eternity, Augustyne and I will ever agree. All the same, as brothers in Jesus we together rejoice that there is great unity in the midst of our diversity—even as Augustyne says, "in essential matters, unity; in non-essential matters, liberty; and in all things, charity." I must say, however, that "in all things charity" is a problem, for it seems to me that the understanding that Augustyne has of human nature inhibits his compassion. Whereas Augustyne is concerned with what he thinks humans should ideally be, my concern is with what humans are—and compassion sees people where they are, not where we think they should be.

(It seems to me that Augustyne thinks that he is humble because he has a perfect understanding of humility. If he was honest, he could pray, "*Lord it's hard to be humble when you're perfect in every way.*"[287] Perhaps, though, I am jealous because God has used Augustyne in such a tremendous way.)

Some of the differences between Augustyne and me come down to the word "perfect." Augustyne thinks of perfection as an untainted reflection of an ideal, and I think of perfection as authentic movement toward an ideal. Perfection is authentically becoming oneself. "Be perfect," said Jesus, "as your father in heaven is perfect." A perfectionist might latch on to this verse and say, "see, we are to be without fault"; but this is not at all what Jesus meant by the word "perfect." "Perfect" and "goal" are here related: a door is perfect insofar as it fulfills the goal for which it was designed—to create a moveable barrier between the inside and the outside; and the hinges of such a door are perfect insofar as they fulfill their goal—to enable the door to open and close freely. The same is true of the perfect person: a perfect person is one who lives in humility; and to live in humility is (knowingly or unknowingly) to live in the teachings of Jesus. (The perfect Logos himself did not become human because he chose to be humble, but he became human because he is humble.)

Being perfect is being full of grace, that virtue which says, "God loves you as you are, and his acceptance of you is not based on becoming better." Like perfection, *grace finds goodness in everything*. It sees beauty in everyone, *however disagreeable or loathsome they might be,* for it is the image of God in every person that grace loves.

Perfection includes an awareness of imperfections. I think of this when I make pottery. When I remove one of my creations from the kiln only to see a crack in it, I don't throw it away—for even in its imperfection it is useful. I pulverize it, add water to it, and mix it with other clay so that it can be used again. While a crack in a cup may undermine the cup, the crack nevertheless reminds me that *light comes into us when we acknowledge that we are broken*, that we need mercy. As painful as it might be, even the pulverization process is beautiful—for within this process we know that the master potter is renewing us, and so *we thank him for battering our hearts*. We know that *he is good*, and that he will "build up what he has torn down." We thus pray with Isaiah, "You are the potter; and we are the clay, the work of your hand."

Perfection, like a river, is ever-changing. My grandson is perfectly himself right now. My daughter told me that my grandson saw a plump woman in the market. Not unlike how he commented on how skinny I was, my grandson approached the heavy woman and honestly said, "You are the fattest woman that I have ever seen." My daughter was terribly embarrassed. She was also angry with my grandson, for she teaches him that if he doesn't have anything nice to say he shouldn't say anything. My grandson is perfectly himself right now; but if he said the same thing years from now, he would not be perfect.

Perfection, like woven material, uses all things to create beauty: the cloth seems to be tangled and knotty on the inside, but all such untidiness is the work of the master-weaver who seamlessly uses all things to create beauty.

Perfection, like the sea, is patient: its usual strategy is akin to the tireless lapping of eternity that carves away the hardest of stones.

Perfection, *like two stones on the surface of still water*, integrates all things. *It drives intersecting ripples on forever—even as they echo the cry of a tiny babe.*

Endnotes

1. Bruce Cockburn, "Cry of a Tiny Babe" (song)
2. Traditional saying regarding Virgin Mary
3. C.S. Lewis, *The Magician's Nephew* (book)
4. Adapted from T.S. Eliot, *Journey of the Magi* (poem)
5. Adapted from Flannery O'Connor, *Greenleaf* (short story)
6. Neil Young, "Out on the Weekend" (song)
7. Adapted from Carmen Bernos de Gasztold, *Prayers from the Ark* (book)
8. Adapted from C.S. Lewis, *The Magician's Nephew* (book); and Queen, "Bohemian Rhapsody" (song)
9. Adapted from Eliza Gilkyson, "Slouching Towards Bethlehem" (song)
10. Adapted from J.K. Rowling, *Harry Potter and the Philosopher's Stone* (book)
11. Adapted from William Shakespeare, *Hamlet* (play)
12. Friedrich Schleiermacher (coined terminology)
13. Adapted from Gordon Lightfoot, "Carefree Highway" (song)
14. Blended from Pierre Simon Laplace (saying); and Voltaire, *The Thee Impostors* (book)
15. Arnold Toynbee, *You Can Pack Up Your Troubles* (article)
16. Blended from C.S. Lewis, *Mere Christianity* (book); and Thomas More, *Utopia* (short story)
17. John Milton, *Paradise Lost* (poem)
18. Barenaked Ladies, "It's All Been Done" (song)
19. U2, "God Part II" (song)
20. Adapted from William Shakespeare, *Romeo and Juliet* (play)
21. Queen, "We Are the Champions" (song)
22. Samuel Beckett, *Waiting for Godot* (play)
23. John 19:28 (book)
24. Adapted from Chinua Achebe, *Things Fall Apart* (book)
25. Pink Floyd, "Damage" (song)
26. Fyodor Dostoyevski, *The Idiot* (book)
27. Blended from Antoine de Saint-Exupéry, *The Little Prince* (book); and Alighieri Dante, *Purgatorio* (canto 18) (poem)
28. Heart, "Magic Man" (song)
29. Rodriguez, "Sugarman" (song)
30. Flannery O'Connor, *View of the Woods* (short story)

31. Bob Dylan, "Precious Angel" (song)
32. Adapted from Galatians 5:6 (book)
33. Antoine de Saint-Exupéry, *The Little Prince* (book)
34. The Beatles, "Girl" (song)
35. Adapted from U2, "When I Look at the World" (song)
36. Radiohead, "Creep" (song)
37. 1 Timothy 4:8 (book)
38. C.S. Lewis, *The Magician's Nephew* (book)
39. Bruce Cockburn, "Lovers in a Dangerous Time" (song)
40. C.S. Lewis, *The Magician's Nephew* (book)
41. Doobie Brothers, "Black Water" (song)
42. Lewis Carroll, *Through the Looking Glass* (book)
43. Blended from Kenneth Grahame, *The Wind in the Willows* (book); and C.S. Lewis, *The Magician's Nephew* (book)
44. U2, "Where the Streets Have No Name" (song)
45. Blended and adapted from 5th Dimension, "Aquarius / Let the Sunshine In" (song); and John Denver, "Sunshine on My Shoulders" (song)
46. Adapted from Therese of Lisieux, *The Story of a Soul* (book)
47. Fyodor Dostoyevski, *The Brothers Karamazov* (Father Zossima) (book)
48. Rush, "New World Man" (song)
49. Neil Young, "There's a World" (song)
50. Bruce Cockburn, "Great Big Love" (song)
51. The Tree of Life (Mrs. O'Brien) (movie)
52. Adapted from Thomas Gray, *Elegy in a Country Church-Yard* (poem)
53. Adapted from William Blake, *Auguries of Innocence* (poem)
54. Adapted from Blaise Pascal, *Pensées* (book)
55. Flannery O'Connor, *The Crop* (short story)
56. Van Morrison, "In the Garden" (song)
57. Cranberries, "Don't Analyze" (song)
58. Adapted from Titus 1:15 (book)
59. Pink Floyd, "Us and Them" (song)
60. The Beatles, "Nowhere Man" (song)
61. Antoine de Saint-Exupéry, *The Little Prince* (book)
62. Mark Twain, *Diary of Eve* (short story)
63. Supertramp, "The Logical Song" (song)
64. Supertramp, "The Logical Song" (song)
65. Blended and adapted from Maltbie Davenport Babcock, "This is My Father's World" (hymn); and Bee Gees, "How Deep is Your Love" (song)
66. Brother Lawrence of the Resurrection, *The Practice of the Presence of God* (book)
67. Cat Stevens, "Moonshadow" (song)
68. Princess Bride (Vizzini) (movie)
69. Blended from Carly Simon, "You're So Vain" (song); and Rodriguez, "Crucify Your Mind" (song)
70. Adapted from Søren Kierkegaard (parable)
71. John Donne, *Holy Sonnet 14* ("Batter My Heart") (poem)
72. Blended and adapted from The Troggs, "Wild Thing" (song); and Rodriguez, "I Think of You" (song)
73. Bob Marley, "Is this Love?" (song)

74. Barenaked Ladies, "Thanks that was Fun" (song)

75. Meatloaf, "Bat Out of Hell" (song)

76. Eric Carmen "All By Myself "(song)

77. Carpenters, "Goodbye to Love" (song)

78. Adapted from Helen Keller (saying)

79. The Guess Who, "American Woman" (song)

80. Meatloaf, "Bat Out of Hell" (song)

81. Marguerite Duras, *Malady of Death* (book)

82. Adapted from Led Zeppelin, "Dazed and Confused" (song)

83. John Donne, *Song* ("Go and Catch a Falling Star") (poem)

84. Desiderius Erasmus, *In Praise of Folly* (book)

85. Flannery O'Connor, *The Barber* (short story)

86. John Milton, *Paradise Lost* (poem)

87. U2, "Stand Up Comedy" (song)

88. Adapted from Rush, "Analog Kid" (song)

89. Fyodor Dostoyevski, *The Brothers Karamazov* (Markel) (book)

90. U2, "Love Rescued Me" (song)

91. Adapted from Leo Tolstoy, *The Death of Ivan Ilyich* (short story)

92. Paul McCartney, "Yesterday" (song)

93. Rodriguez, "Sandrevan Lullaby" (song)

94. Adapted from Samuel Johnson, *Rasselas* (book)

95. Pink Floyd, "Time" (song)

96. T.S. Eliot, *The Wasteland* (poem)

97. Adapted from Steve Miller Band, "Time Keeps on Slipping into the Future" (song)

98. Malcolm Muggeridge, *Chronicles of Wasted Time* (book)

99. Pink Floyd, "Time" (song)

100. Samuel Foote, *The Life of Johnson* (biographical note)

101. Adapted from Søren Kierkegaard (parable)

102. The Beatles, "Nowhere Man" (song)

103. Adapted from The Beatles, "Nowhere Man" (song)

104. Nathaniel Hawthorne, *The Scarlet Letter* (book)

105. Mumford and Sons, "Dustbowl Dance" (song)

106. Blended and adapted from Supertramp, "Logical Song" (song); and George Bernard Shaw, *The Importance of Being Earnest* (play)

107. T.S. Eliot, *Hollow Men* (poem)

108. John Donne, Meditation 17 ("Devotions upon Emergent Occasions") (poem)

109. Elton John, "Don't Let the Sun Go Down on Me" (song)

110. Blended and adapted from *Hymn to Demeter* (book); and Luke 2:35 (book)

111. Lewis Carroll, *Alice in Wonderland* (book)

112. Lewis Carroll, *Alice in Wonderland* (book)

113. Kenneth Grahame, *The Wind in the Willows* (book)

114. Adapted from Pink Floyd, "Brick in the Wall" (song)

115. U2, "Wake Up Dead Man" (song)

116. Pink Floyd, "Hero's Return" (song)

117. John Bunyan, *Pilgrim's Progress* (book)

118. George Bernard Shaw, *The Importance of Being Earnest* (play)

119. Eric Clapton, "Before You Accuse Me" (song)

120. Blended and adapted from Ralph Waldo Emerson, *Self-Reliance* (book); Leonard

Cohen, "Anthem" (song); and Alighieri Dante, *Purgatorio* (canto 7) (poem)

121. Adapted from Ambrose Bierce, *The Devil's Dictionary* (book)
122. Pierre Teilhard de Chardin, *The Divine Milieu* (book)
123. Pink Floyd, "In the Flesh" (song)
124. William Shakespeare, *As You Like It* (Jaques) (play)
125. Adapted from William Shakespeare, *Macbeth* (Macbeth) (play)
126. Adapted from Pink Floyd, "The Show Must Go On" (song)
127. Adapted from Ambrose Bierce, *The Devil's Dictionary* (book)
128. Rodriguez, "Like Janis" (song)
129. Adapted from Blaise Pascal, *Pensées* (book)
130. Adapted from Hans Christian Andersen, *The Emperor's New Clothes* (fable)
131. Adapted from Supertramp, "Crime of the Century" (song)
132. Bob Dylan, "Precious Angel" (song)
133. Adapted from U2, "Moment of Surrender" (song)
134. Adapted from Martin Buber, *I and Thou* (book)
135. Supertramp, "From Now On" (song)
136. Adapted from Albert E. Brumley, "I'll Fly Away" (hymn)
137. John Milton, *Paradise Lost* (poem)
138. Bette Midler, "From a Distance" (song)
139. Adapted from Dietrich Bonhoeffer, *Letters and Papers from Prison* (book)
140. Adapted from U2, "Peace on Earth" (song)
141. Bruce Cockburn, "Lovers in a Dangerous Time" (song)
142. Adapted from Mahatma Gandhi, *My Experiments with Truth* (book)
143. Jim Elliot (journal entry)
144. Adapted from William Shakespeare's *Hamlet* (Marcellus) (play)
145. Blended and adapted from J.J. Kale, "Hard to Thrill" (song); and Queen, "Bohemian Rhapsody" (song)
146. Samuel Johnson, *Rasselas* (book)
147. Bob Dylan, "Blowin' in the Wind" (song)
148. Bob Dylan, "Blowin' in the Wind" (song)
149. Paul Tillich, *Systematic Theology* (book)
150. Bachman-Turner Overdrive, "Lookin' Out for Number One" (song)
151. The Beatles, "I am the Walrus" (song)
152. U2, "One" (song)
153. Adapted from Victor Hugo, *Les Misérables* (book)
154. Buce Cockburn, "Gospel of Bondage" (song)
155. John Donne, *Holy Sonnet 14* ("Batter My Heart") (poem)
156. Blended and adapted from Supertramp, "Rudy" (song); and Fleetwood Mac, "No Questions Asked" (song)
157. American Beauty (Ricky Fitts) (movie)
158. Blended and adapted from Alighieri Dante, *Purgatorio* (canto 30) (poem); and Maltbie Davenport Babcock, "This is My Father's World" (hymn)
159. John Denver, "Annie's Song" (song)
160. John Denver, "Annie's Song" (song)
161. Desiderius Erasmus, *In Praise of Folly* (book)
162. Fyodor Dostoyevski, *The Idiot* (Prince Muishkin) (book)
163. C.S. Lewis, *The Lion, the Witch, and the Wardrobe* (book)
164. Led Zeppelin

165. Blaise Pascal, *Pensées* (book)

166. Samuel Beckett, *Waiting for Godot* (play)

167. Ludwig Wittgenstein, *Tractatus 7* (book)

168. Blended and adapted from U2, "I'll Go Crazy if I Don't Go Crazy Tonight" (song); and Bob Dylan, "Precious Angel" (song)

169. Minnie Riperton, "Lovin' You" (song)

170. Adapted from Jesus Christ Superstar (Mary Magdalene) (movie/rock opera)

171. Adapted from S. Trevor Francis, "O the Deep, Deep Love of Jesus" (hymn)

172. Adapted from Fleetwood Mac, "Sarah" (song)

173. Adapted from Thomas Merton, *The Seven Storey Mountain* (book)

174. Saint Augustine, *Confessions* (book)

175. Pink Floyd, "Money" (song)

176. Bruce Cockburn, "Call it Democracy" (song)

177. U2, "God II" (song)

178. Adapted from Mother Theresa of Calcutta (saying)

179. U2, "Tryin' to Throw Your Arms Around the World" (song)

180. Mother Theresa of Calcutta (saying)

181. Fyodor Dostoyevski, *The Brothers Karamazov* (book)

182. Ben Hur (chain-gang scene) (movie)

183. Sinnéad O'Connor, "Thank You for Hearing Me" (song)

184. Alighieri Dante, *Inferno* (canto 23) (poem)

185. Pink Floyd, "Comfortably Numb" (song)

186. John Newton, "Amazing Grace" (hymn)

187. Adapted from Pink Floyd, "Empty Spaces" (song)

188. Simon and Garfunkel, "Sound of Silence" (song)

189. Cat Stevens, "Back Home" (song)

190. Simon and Garfunkel, "The Sound of Silence" (song)

191. U2, "Love Rescued Me" (song)

192. Adapted from Therese of Lisieux, *The Story of a Soul* (book)

193. Blended and adapted from Bruce Cockburn, "Somebody Touched Me" (song); and Bill Gaither, "He Touched Me" (hymn)

194. Bruce Cockburn, "Wondering Where the Lions Are" (song)

195. Adapted from Corrie ten Boom, *The Hiding Place* (book)

196. Gottfried Leibniz, *The Monadology* (book)

197. Leo Tolstoy, *God Sees the Truth, But Waits* (short story)

198. Pink Floyd, "The Trial" (song)

199. Nathaniel Hawthorne, *Young Goodman Brown* (short story)

200. Rodriguez, "'Cause" (song)

201. Fyodor Dostoyevski, *The Brothers Karamazov* (Father Zossima) (book)

202. Mahatma Gandhi, *The Story of My Experiments with Truth* (book)

203. Blended and adapted from Leonard Cohen, "Diamonds in the Mine" (song); Joni Mitchell, "Paved Paradise" (song); and J.R.R. Tolkien, *The Lord of the Rings* (Treebeard) (book)

204. Blended and adapted from Leonard Cohen, "Diamonds in the Mine" (song); and C.S. Lewis, *The Lion, the Witch, and the Wardrobe* (book).

205. Blended and adapted from Neil Young, "Comes a Time" (song); and U2, "Peace on Earth" (song)

206. Robert Robinson, "Come Thou Fount of Every Blessing" (hymn)

207. Florence and the Machine, "Big God" (song)

208. Inspired by Ben Hur (carrying the cross scene) (movie)

209. Adapted from Prayer of St. Francis

210. Blended and adapted from Rodriguez, "Crucify Your Mind" (song); and Simone Weil, *Waiting for God* (book)

211. The Matrix (Morpheus) (movie)

212. John Donne, *Hymn to God, My God, in My Sickness* (poem)

213. Adapted from "Were You There When They Crucified My Lord?" (spiritual)

214. U2, "Love Rescued Me" (song)

215. Bruce Cockburn, "Cry of a Tiny Babe" (song)

216. Søren Kierkegaard, *The Crowd is Untruth* (book)

217. Leonard Cohen, "Hallelujah" (song)

218. Much of this paragraph is an adaptation from Bernard of Clairvaux, *On the Love of God* (book)

219. Sting, "Russians" (song)

220. Pink Floyd, "The Gunner's Dream" (song)

221. Adapted from Supertramp, "Crime of the Century" (song)

222. Alighieri Dante, *Purgatorio* (canto 28) (poem)

223. Adapted from C.S. Lewis, *The Abolition of Man* (book)

224. Malcolm Muggeridge, *Something Beautiful for God* (book)

225. Adapted from U2, "Until the End of the World" (song)

226. Adapted from Søren Kierkegaard (parable)

227. Lewis Carroll, *Alice in Wonderland* (book)

228. Bee Gees, "Islands in the Stream" (song)

229. Pink Floyd, "Waiting for the Worms" (song)

230. Pink Floyd, "Is There Anybody Out There?" (song)

231. The Guess Who, "Humpty's Blues" (song)

232. Alighieri Dante, *Purgatorio* (canto 11) (poem)

233. The Beatles, "Nowhere Man" (song)

234. Adapted from Mumford and Sons, "The Cave" (song)

235. Carpenters, "Goodbye to Love" (song)

236. J.R.R. Tolkien, *The Return of the King* (book)

237. Blended and adapted from William Shakespeare's *Hamlet* (Ophelia) (play); and Pink Floyd, "Goodbye Cruel World" (song)

238. Pink Floyd, "Two Suns in the Sunset" (song)

239. Adapted from America, "A Horse with No Name" (song)

240. Adapted from Jean-Paul Sartre, *No Exit* (play)

241. Alighieri Dante, *Inferno* (canto 1) (poem)

242. Blended and adapted from Robert Frost, *The Road Not Taken* (poem); and Kenneth Grahame, *The Wind in the Willows* (book)

243. Unknown author, *Everyman* (play)

244. Robert Frost, *The Road Not Taken* (poem)

245. T.S. Eliot, *Journey of the Magi* (poem)

246. Pulp Fiction (Jewels) (movie)

247. U2, "Beautiful Day" (song)

248. Adapted from Fyodor Dostoyevski, *The Brothers Karamazov* (book)

249. Adapted from Rolling Stones, "You Can't Always Get What You Want" (song) and "(I Can't Get No) Satisfaction" (song).

250. U2, "Grace" (song)

251. Adapted from Alfred Lord Tennyson, *In Memoriam* A.H.H. Obiit 1833: 96 (eulogy)

252. Mumford and Sons, "Winter Winds" (song)

253. John A.T. Robinson, *Honest to God* (book)

254. Blended and adapted from Mark 4:36–41 (book); U2, "Please" (song); and Led Zeppelin, "When the Levee Breaks" (song)

255. John Bunyan, *Pilgrim's Progress* (book)

256. Karl Rahner (coined terminology)

257. Adapted from C.S. Lewis, *The Problem of Pain* (book)

258. Adapted from Bruce Cockburn, "Call it Democracy" (song)

259. Bruce Cockburn, "Call it Democracy" (song)

260. Adapted from U2, "Peace on Earth" (song)

261. Karl Marx, *A Contribution to the Critique of Hegel's Philosophy of Right* (book)

262. Friedrich Nietzsche, *The Gay Science* (book)

263. Adapted from U2, "The Wanderer" (song)

264. U2, "Mysterious Ways" (song)

265. Theodore Rebard (attribution)

266. Saint Augustine, *Confessions* (book)

267. Janice Joplin, "Ball and Chain" (song)

268. Bee Gees, "More Than a Woman" (song)

269. Meatloaf, "Heaven Can Wait" (song)

270. Blended and adapted from Boston, "Foreplay" (song); and Led Zeppelin, "Dazed and Confused" (song)

271. Martin Luther (traditional attribution)

272. The Guess Who, "No Time" (song)

273. John Donne, *A Hymn to God the Father* (poem)

274. Saint Augustine (traditional attribution)

275. Adapted from Antoine de Saint-Exupéry, *The Little Prince* (book)

276. Bruce Cockburn, "Wondering Where the Lions Are" (song)

277. Blaise Pascal, *Pensées* (book)

278. Blended from Bob Dylan, "Rolling Stone" (song) and Barenaked Ladies, "Shoe box" (song)

279. Adapted from Goodwill Hunting (parkbench scene) (movie)

280. Adapted from The Sound of Music (gazebo scene) (movie)

281. U2, "Babyface" (song)

282. Alighieri Dante, *Inferno* (canto 34) (poem)

283. Blended and adapted from Bruce Cockburn, "One of the Best Ones" (song); and U2, "Beautiful Day" (song)

284. The Cranberries, "Analyse" (song)

285. Adapted from Karl Marx, *Theses on Feuerbach* (book)

286. Adapted from Thomas à Kempis, *The Imitation of Christ* (book)

287. Adapted from Willie Nelson, "It's Hard to be Humble" (song)